White Lies,
Black Dare

Joanna Nadin

LITTLE, BROWN BOOKS FOR YOUNG READERS
www.lbkids.co.uk

LITTLE, BROWN BOOKS FOR YOUNG READERS

First published in Great Britain in 2016 by Hodder & Stoughton

1 3 5 7 9 10 8 6 4 2

A CIP catalogue record for this book
is available from the British Library.

ISBN 978-0-349124-53-7

Typeset in Bembo by M Rules
Printed and bound in Great Britain by
Clays Ltd, St Ives plc

The paper and board used in this book are
made from wood from responsible sources.

MIX
Paper from
responsible sources
FSC® C104740
www.fsc.org

Little, Brown Books for Young Readers
An imprint of
Hachette Children's Group
Part of Hodder & Stoughton
Carmelite House
50 Victoria Embankment
London EC4Y 0DZ

An Hachette UK Company
www.hachette.co.uk

www.hachettechildrens.co.uk

"Poignant, fu_ny, and _____ _oe _l Alone paints a picture of child poverty, neglect and ab_se that is somehow life-affirm__g and heart_____ _____ _ile it will break your hea_t. The brigh__ _oloured cast of characters, from Otis the Jamaican bus-driver to Asha the girl with a big imagination and heart to match, contrast with the grim, grey reality of life for a thirteen year old kid trying to survive on a tough inner city estate. But it is Joe himself – brave, clever, resilient but also vulnerable and broken – who readers will fall in love with. There is a beautiful simplicity and lyricism to this book which make it incredibly moving and I absolutely loved it!" Catherine Bruton

"A real boy's voice, nailed hard to a tale rich with wrong decisions, hopeless plans and stabs at redemption. I loved it." Steve Cole

"Frightening and funny, bleak and tender, serious and surprising, *Joe All Alone* is a gem of a book that catches the heart and lifts the spirits (just like a flock of parakeets in Peckham!)" Tanya Landman

"A gripping, heart-warming contemporary story about a young teenager forced to make difficult decisions in order to survive." Book Trust

"Deeply poignant, deceptively simple, this book will cut the reader to the bone almost without their realising it." Imogen Russell-Williams, teensonmoonlane.co.uk

"This book highlights the best and worst of humanity while tackling these highs and lows from the beautiful, naive, vulnerable perspective of a child. A fascinating and heart-warming read for teen readers *Joe All Alone* will leave you longing to protect Joe and give him a big hug and you may learn to appreciate a few things about yourself and your parents that you hadn't noticed before." Laura Iredale, welovethisbook.com

Also by Joanna Nadin
Joe All Alone

For Millie.
May she have Asha's imagination,
heart, and courage.

Truth or Dare?

I thought it was an easy question. Obvious. Like asking, "Would you rather win the final of *The X Factor* or lick the bin outside Maccy D's?" Or, "Do you want fries with that?" Like, duh.

'Cause the truth's dull. It's school uniform and scuffed shoes and the smell of cheap sausages. It's no-label, own-brand, knock-off. Truth's your mum got sick and you had to move in with your not-even-grandpa and you don't go to private school no more. Who wants that? It's stories that glitter. The stuff on telly and in magazines and books: *Harry Potter* and *The Hunger Games* and *School for Stars*. That's why I chose what I did – why I hung round with Angel and Kelly in the first place. Because they had stories and adventure in them, so strong I could see it. Because they knew how to tell tall tales, and how to dream big. Real big. Because you never knew what was going to happen next. Being with them – even just in that Blu-Tack-covered bedroom on Ephraim Street, or on the wall outside Crackerjack – was like a free pass at Peckham Fair. Like all-you-can-eat candyfloss and doughnuts then getting spun on the waltzers until you don't know if you're going to scream or puke and you don't even care which.

Until you do.

It's only now I see it. That dares are dangerous. But telling the truth, that's the biggest risk of all. 'Cause truth is the blade of a knife. Truth is the red circle of shame.

Dares can damage deeper than you imagined. And telling lies can ruin lives. But take it from me, telling the truth's no easy ride. And that first term at the Academy, I did all three.

One

Everyone's got something to say about it. About why moving from Essex to Peckham's going to be a good thing. Otis says we're back where we belong – me and Mum – back where we come from. My friend Joe, he's dead happy because I'm only a few miles away now, so we can see each other more often. More than just the odd Sunday, he says. Even Mrs Joyful King from downstairs has got an opinion. She seen it in Otis's horoscope, she reckons good times are coming. And you got to believe horoscopes. Last month mine told me I was going to reap financial rewards from a canny investment and I ended up winning a pound in a bet over how long Charlie Bardwell could kiss Jonno Everett for, which was only four minutes twenty-three seconds, which is way shorter than Casey Collins and Luke Patmore's brother, which is what I said.

It's only Mum who's got nothing but bad words about it. She says Otis's flat's going to be too small for all of us. That the school's going to be shameful compared to Queen Mary's. That I'll end up with a bunch of no-hopers for friends.

She's doing it now, sat in the back of the taxi parked outside Lyndhurst Villas. Not with words this time, but I can tell by the way her eyes narrow when she sees the grass not mown and the bins not emptied and the world not all rosy like it was before.

Beggars can't be choosers, I want to say, but I don't. 'Cause having to beg is what she's angry about. 'Cause she's the one that's gone and got cancer. She's the one whose boyfriend left her. She's the one who said income insurance was a scam, only then she got no money to pay the rent and no Ellis to pick up the pieces or clear up the puke from chemo and so here we are, moving back in with her step-dad in the flat she was brought up in. Because, yeah, it's not like we was made in Chelsea or anything like that. I went to primary down Bellenden Road round the corner. It was only when Mum got made a barrister that she decided we were too good for round here and dragged me to Epping, where dogs don't poo on the doorstep and no one swears and unicorns play on streets paved with gold. Yeah, right.

She opens her purse, pulls out two twenties – the last of this week's sick benefit, only she don't call it that, 'cause benefits are for other people. Just like cancer was supposed to be and all.

The driver opens the door for her, offers her his arm. She ignores it. "I'm all right," she says. "I'm fine."

He flicks a look at me but I got no answer, I can't speak for her. She's got all the fine words, the truth.

7

All I got is stories from books and films and stuff out of magazines; the same stuff she's always telling me's going to get me nowhere. "You got to focus, Asha," she says. "Focus on facts. That's what matters. That's what makes you money. Facts not fiction."

Money, that's what matters. To her anyway. The way she talks about it like it's magic beans that build you a giant beanstalk to get up and out of your sorry little life. Only look where that got her. No ogre, maybe, but no gold either and we're back down the bottom of the stalk on our backsides. Look where it got Joe and all back when I met him. He's living with his mum now, up in a new flat, and he goes to a new school and all. But it was money his mum was chasing when she left him on his own for two weeks – a thirteen-year-old kid who can't barely use the cooker – before he ended up in care for months. It was money the Dooleys were chasing when they started banging on his door at night. Money Perry Fletcher was chasing when he beat Joe up so bad he couldn't hardly see.

Money's not everything, I want to say. *Nor's facts.*

But I don't, do I? I just drag our bags out and go and ring the bell and wait for Otis, like he's the fairy godfather who can fix everything.

He can't fix school, though. Can't magic up Mallory Towers in the middle of the market. Can't even find me a place at Haberdashers' down New Cross, the only school for miles that gets grades that don't turn Mum's lips into nothing or make your bank balance disappear. So it's the Academy, with the rest of the kids off the estates.

Anyway, like I say, beggars can't be choosers, so no point complaining my skirt's too tight and my shoes are the wrong colour and I don't like the cheese in my sandwiches that much, I'd rather have chips from the canteen. Better to concentrate on the good stuff. I read that in a magazine. You got to see the good in every situation. Like, if you're on a diet, like Casey Collins was for two weeks in Year Seven until she got into fake nails instead, not being allowed to have a Mars bar is rubbish. But then one little square of chocolate is a treat, innit. That's the pearl in the oyster.

And I got a pearl. Patience Williams. She may be a happy-clapper down her dad's church, and she may shop in Plus 14 down Lewisham market instead of up West, but she can dance like Beyoncé when her mum's not looking and she's read every Jacqueline Wilson, in order. Besides, she's the only one who bothered to message back when I said I was moving. So she's all I got. At least that's what I thought at lunchtime when I sat down next to her that first day.

I used to think the playground was where the important stuff got decided – not like who's top of the class, but who's king, or queen, who's their court, and who's just nobody. But once you've passed hopscotch and handstand wonderland, the canteen's what counts, that's where rules get decided and places divided, and this one's no exception.

It's like a test, what you pick to eat, then where you pick to eat it. 'Cause you're a fool if you think you can just sit anywhere. Some seats got no-go signs on them 'cause they're hot, they're wanted; some 'cause no one would sit there even if the prize was a trip up Westfield with a no-limit credit card. I know where I want to sit, one day. But for now, I settle for five tables down to the left, away from the boys chucking chips like they're scoring baskets, away from the girls bragging and braying like they're the stars they want to be. I settle for a plastic chair that's been bagsied already with an outsize blazer and a two-seasons-ago lunchbox. The seat next to Patience. I slip in like it's made me for me, just waiting. And there we are again, like we used to be down primary. Her with her plastic tub of pasta salad and her Jaffa Cakes and juice, and me with my cheese sandwich and my banana and my bottle of water. Misfits, both of us. The fat Christian and the new girl.

"How was Spanish?" she asks.

"*Bueno*," I answer. "Totally *bueno*. 'Cept the only

place left is next to some kid whose fingernails are bleeding, which, like, what is that about? Plus he don't smell good."

"Darryl Benson," Patience says through a mouthful of pasta. She don't eat pretty and I reckon I can teach her about that. I read it in a magazine: talking with your mouth full is one of the Top Ten Turn-Offs For Boys, after bad breath and hairy armpits.

I swallow my sandwich. "Maybe," I say. "I reckon he's a vampire, only he's too kind to bite other people so he just sucks blood from the tips of his fingers. And he can't take a shower because vampires are allergic to water, innit."

But Patience won't play the game.

"*Holy* water," she says. "They're only allergic if it's holy and I don't think they pump that out of the tap. Anyway, vampires aren't real. He just bites his nails, that's all."

"Whatever. He so needs some Lynx."

Then I remember what we used to do.

"Want to swap?" I offer, holding out my brown banana.

"If you like," she says.

I almost choke on her kindness. "Seriously? You'd swap this for a Jaffa Cake?"

"Two." She smiles. "I don't mind, really."

Fool girl, I think, but I do the swap before she changes her mind. And I'm so busy licking chocolate off the top of the orangey bit and thinking I've totally won the lunch-swap lottery, I don't notice the girl who's turned up at our table with her hands on her hips and her hair gelled into zigzags and her ginger sidekick staring green-eyed daggers at Patience. They look like trouble with a capital T. And I feel my heart start banging like I'm climbing on the roller coaster. But I know better than to let them see that.

"I know who you are," says the gelled girl.

"I doubt it," I reply, still licking the biscuit.

"Yeah, I do. You went off to Hogwarts or somewhere. That fancy school."

I see heads turn on next-door tables and eyes fix on me, feel the cheese sandwich in my stomach start to swirl. "Maybe."

"Asha, innit. Asha Wright. You don't know who I am?" She says it like she's a film star, or planning to be one.

I look at her up close now. I do sort of recognise her: the way her mouth half smiles, half sneers; the only-just uniform she's wearing; those massive eyes, ringed by falsies, even though they're banned. Not off the telly, though. From before. And then I see her, queening it in the playground, jumping elastics with her blonde hair down to her backside and her skinny legs flying way higher than any of us, and don't she know it.

"Angel Jones," I say.

"Don't wear it out," she says. But she's not mad at me. She's known. She's somebody. And that's what counts. All that counts, maybe. "So why're you back? Failed your dragon-taming class or summink?"

Her sidekick laughs and I can see she's got a black

tooth and I'm wondering if it's because she drinks too much Coke or if she had a fight, over a boy, and now it's a dead tooth, only she keeps it as a sign to enemies that she's hard, that you don't mess with her.

Patience nudges me and I realise Angel's waiting for an answer and she's not going to take "no comment".

"Something like that," I reply. And then it just comes out. I don't even have to think that hard. And I don't know why I do it except that who wants to hear some sob story about cancer and Mum getting sacked so she can't pay the school fees and even with a scholarship it's two hours on the bus and tube. So instead what comes out is: "There was this boy, total Prince Harry type, you know. Only not ginger, blond; so blond his hair's almost see-through. And rich; his dad is Lord Something. Anyway, we're in detention, just me and him, in the library which is all paintings and the smell of books. And there's just this feeling. It's electric, you know?" I glance at Angel and she nods, like yeah, she knows. "Anyway, the teacher gets called out – Mr Griffin, that's his name – and then we're all over each other. And this goes on for, like, weeks. We get detention deliberately so we can be together. But then his dad finds out and tells my mum and they go all Montague and Capulet on us and ban us from seeing each other because his dad's got him set to marry someone from Chelsea. And now he's in Scotland and I'm back here, innit."

I wait for my audience to react. Because that's what it's about – being somebody, being seen. No point doing anything if there's no one there to watch you do it. I saw that on a film.

The sidekick's first. "Liar," she says.

"You reckon?" I say. "There's loads I could tell you about that place. It's proper stuck-up. I'm glad to be rid."

"Is that true?" asks Patience.

"What, about Parker – that's his name, Parker, did I say that? – or that I'm glad to be back?"

"Both," she says.

"Course," I say. And it's only half a lie.

Then I look up at Angel, who still hasn't spoken. Right then her name suits her. Her hair's a halo in the strip lights of the canteen and she's so above us all she almost flies.

She pushes her tongue into the wad of gum that's her lunch and blows a fat bubble that snaps and disappears behind her Rimmel-glossed lips. Then she looks at me, like she's drinking me in, testing me out for flavour, seeing if I'm sweet or poison. And though all she says is, "See you around, Ash," I know I've passed. I'm in. And then it's like fairground lights start to flash and a bell rings and I hear the clatter of wheels on a wooden track. Because I can feel it beginning. Feel it lurch out of the gate and down the first steep swoop. I'm on a roller coaster. I'm on the ride of my life and I don't want to get off, even if I could.

Two

"Who was that other girl?" I ask.

Me and Patience are idling down Rye Lane, drinking cans of fake Coke she got us with her tuck money in Crackerjack, taking turns to kick an empty fag packet.

"The ginger one?"

"Yeah, her with the tooth."

"That's Kelly. They're always in trouble, her and Angel. Mr Goater – he's the Deputy Head, only everyone calls him Bloater – had them in detention for a whole week once because they pierced this Year Seven girl's ear in the toilets. She said she wanted them to, but I think they just told her to say that. You want to stay well away."

"All right, Mum," I say.

"I didn't mean it like that," she says quickly, even though I'm smiling. "Mr Goater's all right really. You just got to know what kind of mood he's in."

"Kelly what?" I ask.

"Huh?"

"You know, her surname. Like Williams or Wright or, I don't know, Chumley-flipping-Warner."

"Oh, that. It's nothing double-barrelled. As if. It's Dooley," Patience says. "She's a Dooley."

And when she says it – Dooley – I feel something inside me flip and flounder. Because, even though I've not lived here for three years, I know what that name means. And more than that, what it means to Joe. All right, so it was his mum's boyfriend Dean he was scared of, and Dean who still gives him nightmares now – getting early release and turning up at the new flat, persuading his mum he's a new man after all. But the Dooleys are the ones Dean ran with. The Dooleys chasing a debt is the reason Joe got left on his own when his mum ran off with Dean. And Joe's the reason one of the Dooleys is inside now.

But Kelly might not be one of his kids, I think – the one Joe grassed, I mean. Or maybe just a distant cousin. Though she got the hair. And that look that's like she's up to something, or thinking about it. Maybe I just won't tell Joe I met her. Not yet anyway. Not 'til I know who she really is and what that means. Besides, if she finds out who I am she might not want to know me anyway. Not that I could tell her, 'cause I don't know who I am to Joe, not really. Friend, sure. Girlfriend? Once upon a time I thought so, or thought that's what I wanted. But I reckon he's more like a brother now. A lanky, white, weird brother. And I laugh when I think that, but in a good way, 'cause *he's* good.

"You want to come in?" Patience asks. We're outside her house now – the vicarage, though it's nothing like the ones in books, you know, all grey and ivy-covered with headless ghosts in the attic. This one's red-brick with plastic windows and a *Jesus Loves You* rainbow sticker on the door. No ghosts in there I reckon. Just God and cats and the smell of saltfish.

"Nah, you're all right. I got to get back, innit."

I don't. 'Cause what is there to get back to? Only I don't want to hang round Patience too much, 'cause it might put Angel off, like she'll know if I've been in there 'cause the smell of Jesus will stick to me.

"See you tomorrow, then?" she asks. "At school."

"Course," I say. "Where else would I go?"

Patience shrugs. "I don't know." She pauses, then adds, "I'm glad you're back."

"Yeah," I say. "Me too."

And I am. Right up until I get to our flats, walk up the stairs past Mrs Joyful King, and the Patels, and

21

the Polish men who change every month, and in our front door. Where the truth hits me almost as hard as the sorry silence, but for the tick-tock of my almost-grandfather's clock, counting down the minutes until the next pill.

Welcome home, Asha.

Cancer's not like it is in magazines or on *Holby*. On telly you can't smell the sick or the staleness from lying in bed too long. You can't feel the sadness that seeps into the sofa and the curtains so that as you walk by it brushes off on you even if you're singing at the time. Telly's a lie, a beautiful one. In here, cancer's only ugly.

Seeing her lying there, on a made-up bed in front of the telly at four in the afternoon, it's like seeing The Wicked Witch of the West taking up bingo or something. Or maybe not a witch, but some bigwig, innit. She used to be invincible, nothing could stop her. Not the crappy ex who run off to Birmingham before his daughter was even born. Not the dad who said she was wasting her time with law school and what she really wanted was a job down Shaniqua's doing weaves and manicures. Not the criminals who would stare poison at her across the courtroom, or their families who would spit at her patent shoes outside. Only now look at her. She's pathetic. Like a sick tiger, and I don't know what to do around it. How to be. If it needs petting or if it'll bite.

"How was it?" she asks.

"All right," I say. "Where's Otis?"

"At work. He'll be back to make tea." She sighs, like even talking is too much to bear, shifts her weight on the bed. "Tell me about the teachers."

"They're fine."

She raises an eyebrow that used to be plucked and now's just drawn on.

"Honest," I say. "This guy we had for history – Robinson – he did this rhyme for all the kings and queens so we could remember them. It was great."

"*Mr* Robinson. And you already know all the kings and queens. So should the rest of the class."

"I know, but—"

"It's not for ever, anyway," she says. "As soon as a place opens at Haberdashers' you can transfer."

"I don't see what's so wrong with the Academy," I say.

"You want a list, chile?" she asks, lapsing into her old person voice. The voice of her mum, of Otis.

"You did all right," I point out.

"I took the long way, the hard way. You don't want that, believe me."

I look at her, lying there. Look where the long, hard way got her. Right back where she started. That's why she's so angry. Because she escaped and now she's been dragged back. "No shame in coming home," says Otis. But there is, for her. She don't belong here with the nylon carpet all psychedelic swirls, the fake-gold picture frames, the reggae on the radio. She belongs somewhere else, with wooden floors and white sheets and white man's music on a thousand-pound stereo. She thinks she was born to the wrong family, innit. I used to think that too, about me. Used to imagine I was adopted and that my real mum and dad were famous actors and one day they'd roll up in a sports car and take me to Hollywood and I'd be a child star and live in hotels and eat corn dogs and drink root beer. That my life would be diamond instead of the dull chip of mica it is.

I'm still waiting.

"You make any friends?" she asks when the silence gets too hard to bear.

"Remember Patience?" I say. And I tell Mum about her. That she's in my tutor group and in my English and maths classes. That we sat next to each other at lunch and walked home together. And that she's got two cats called Matthew and Mark, which are really dumb names for cats, if you think about it, even if they are from the gospel.

"So her father's still the preacher?"

I nod, taking a peanut out of the bowl that's sat untouched in front of her since Otis left it this morning.

"That's good."

"I s'pose."

"Anyone else?" she asks.

I throw the peanut in the air and catch it in my mouth, and the crowd in my head goes wild. I shake my head as I chew. "Nah. Not yet."

Because that list she talked about, about what's wrong with the Academy? Angel Jones would be the cherry on top of it.

Joe's full of questions too. He calls after dinner, all, "Is Miss Burton still there?" and, "Have you got Bloater for geography?" and, "Did you see Perry Fletcher?"

"I don't know," I answer to the first question. Then, "No, someone called Watson." And, "He's in Fourways now, Patience says. 'Cause of what he done to you and also 'cause he put some midget kid called Franco in the bins, you know, the food ones, right over his head."

I don't tell him about Angel, either. Nor Kelly

26

Dooley. Like I say, I know what he'd think and I don't think I want to hear it. Not 'til I have to.

"I can't wait to see you," he says then. "Sunday, yeah?"

I wonder what Angel's doing Sunday. Patience'll be in church. All day, maybe. But Angel doesn't look like she prays down St John's or Latter Rain or any other chapel. She looks like she worships somewhere else entirely.

"Yeah, Sunday," I say. "Can't wait."

But for the first time since we met, a tiny part of me — so tiny it's smaller even than an amoeba on a flea, but real all the same — thinks I can wait. Not 'cause I don't want to see him, I do. But 'cause I want to see her more. Because she'll sparkle. She's diamond. And if I'm with her, maybe my life will turn out to be too.

Three

I walk to school with Patience. I don't plan to, but she's there on the wall waiting when I come down with my bag full of books and my head full of sleep and my piece of toast between my teeth. Her face radiates hope – the same look Joe always has – and I bet myself Angel never needs to look so desperate.

"D'you watch *Eastenders* last night?" I ask, licking the jam off so I've got a mouthful of just strawberries and butter.

"No. We're not allowed. And that is disgusting," she says.

"That's what you think," I say. "But you'll never know until you try." I take a bite of the toast but it's soggy now and I drop the rest in the gutter.

"You could get done for that," Patience says quietly.

"Biodegradable, innit. I'm returning it to the earth. I should get thanked, not done."

She can't say anything to that so we walk through the school gates in silence and that's when I see them, leaning against the fence, their hair trailing through the bars as they hold court with a bunch of older boys I don't know and my mum would say I don't want to. Angel's shirt's a size too small, deliberately I reckon, and one of the boys is staring straight down it. And she just smiles like she knows what's got his attention and it's not her smart talk. Mum would hate that. Patience hates that.

"She's going to end up in Fourways too, the way she's going," she says.

I watch as Angel raises her arms above her head so her belly's out, then busts a move.

"Seriously," adds Patience.

"Did anyone ever tell you you sound like your mama?" I ask.

Patience looks at me as if I've just slapped her.

"Joke!" I say.

But part of me's not joking. And the rest is too busy wondering what Angel might do to end up in in a referral unit. And hoping I get to watch.

All morning Patience sticks to me like I'm flypaper. In maths she's saved me a seat down the front, a seat I reckon's been empty all year, 'cause who'd want to be that near Mrs Gupta? At lunch we sit with a bunch of her friends from Year Nine, all happy-clappers. Some kid called Dennis who looks like he's already practising law, he's got his glasses and his shiny, shiny shoes and his briefcase. And two other girls who smile so much it must make their faces ache. They're talking about this trip they're going on, to Southend, and I'm nodding and saying "totally" like I'm into God and Jesus and Holy flaming Mary, but really I'm looking behind them to the canteen, where Angel's chewing a single fry and watching me with this smile on her face like she's the Cheshire cat. And I wonder if I'm the mouse, or Alice.

It don't take long to find out.

In English, the seat next to Patience is taken by Dennis, who slaps his briefcase down before I can bags it. So I'm on my own again, scanning the room for the least worst option – i.e. not at the front 'cause I don't want to look like a keener and not at the back 'cause I don't want to look like a waster and definitely not next to Darryl Benson – when a voice says, "Over 'ere."

And there she is, back to the window so she's in a halo of sunshine, living up to her name.

Angel.

There's a spare seat on the end of her table, between Kelly and the aisle. But that's not mine.

"Budge up," she says. And Kelly, who's chewing

gum like it's a sport and she's up for gold, sighs and moves one seat over so I can slip right between them like the jam in a sandwich.

"Thanks," I say.

"*De nada*," says Angel.

"You do Spanish?" I ask. "I didn't see you."

Angel laughs. "Nah. As if. You only get to do that if you can speak French and why would I need to do that? Got it off this film, innit."

"You might go to Paris one day," I offer. "Some bloke might take you all the way up the Eiffel Tower and propose."

"Like McCardle," sniggers Kelly.

"Shut up," says Angel. "Anyway, he's from Deptford High Street so I wouldn't need no French then neither."

"Who's McCardle?" I ask.

Kelly stretches the gum out of her mouth, a long, pink, shiny string that matches her earrings, then ravels it back in and nods towards the door. "Him."

And in walks this man, only just a man 'cause he

can't be more than twenty-something, his trousers tight and his black hair in tiny dreads; so far from Bloater, who's milk-pale and bursting out his buttons, that they're like two different species.

Almost.

"Dooley, gum, now," the man-boy fires out, *BAM, BAM, BAM,* like he's a sharp shooter and Kelly's the lowlife criminal in his sights.

She sighs again and lugs herself to the front, pulls the wad of gum out her mouth and drops it into the bin he's holding out.

"Anyone else?" He scans the room, his eyes pausing on me. I shake my head, and he nods like he knows I wouldn't lie. But he don't know me at all, I think. Maybe I could have gum, maybe I could have a whole sweetshop in my bag. Maybe.

Four other kids got truth in their mouths, come forward and spit out balls of Juicy Fruit and Double Mint, tutting and soaking up the cheers and jeers as they strut back to their desks.

"All right," says McCardle. "Holiday's over. Back

to books. And whiteboards. And words, all those words, waiting for you sorry souls to ignite them or ignore them, waiting to be waved in joy or protest, or wasted, washed away."

A few kids groan, but not me – I smile. 'Cause he don't talk like a teacher, he talk like a poet or something bigger and better than this place. Something beyond. And I wonder what his story is, if he was once famous like Shakespeare, or if he's waiting to be. Turns out he's thinking the same about us.

"You're twelve, thirteen now. I want to know where you think you'll be when you've lived double that. When you're twenty-five, twenty-six. Finished uni? In a job? Here on the High Road or on King's Road? Or further: Oxford or Cambridge or Cambridge, Massachusetts? What will you be doing? Who will you be?"

"Well I ain't going to be flaming Katy Perry, am I," sneers Kelly.

"Not unless she goes ginger," says some boy, the Gs all hard like in "God".

"All right." McCardle waves his hand like he's patting the air down. "Just use your imaginations. And anyone who puts 'playing centre forward for Chelsea' gets detention. 'Arsenal' you'll get an A-star." He smiles then and I see one of his teeth glint, like a rapper or a pirate or a bad boy from the estate, capped gold to show he got money, got power. But McCardle don't have the look of any of them. He got more the look of Joe. Like he don't quite belong round here. And then I remember something, something I showed Joe once: the parakeets up on the Rye; birds from another country, only they made their paradise here in Peckham. And I think maybe he's like that too. Found his place here. Or back here. That he been away but flew back, migrated.

"I want a page at least," McCardle adds. "You've got half an hour. Go."

Everyone's talking then. Thinking. Dreaming. I glance over at Patience, sucking her biro like it's a lollipop, wondering who she wants to be. Holy Mary, maybe. Or the first woman Archbishop of Wherever.

"I know where I want to be," says Kelly. "I want
to marry some eejit and have five kids by the time
I'm twenty-six and then get fat and wait to die. Oh
no, wait. That's my mum, innit."

Angel laughs, so I do too.

"I ain't staying round 'ere, that's for sure," Angel
says. "Gonna be in Hollywood."

"Like your dad?" asks a girl behind us, only it's not
a proper question, it's a prod, a poke, all dripping in
sarcasm.

"He *is* there," Angel snaps. "And he saw Brad Pitt
last week, got his autograph for me and all, so you
can eff off."

"Angel Jones, that's enough," says McCardle. "I
want to see the words, not hear them. You've only
got twenty-five minutes now and that clock is tick-
tocking the seconds down, tick-tocking your life
away."

"I wish it would flaming hurry up," she says, her
eyes right on him, like she's goading him. Or daring
him to tell her her life's worth more than that.

But he don't give her the satisfaction.

"You're not the only one," he says, not even flinching. "An afternoon with you can seem like a life sentence."

And it's meant to be a joke, I know that, 'cause he's smiling and I can see that tooth again. But Angel ain't smiling. Her face is nothing but scowl and blush-red that got nothing to do with Rimmel and everything to do with humiliation. I want to ask her about her dad: if he's really in Hollywood, if he's an actor or a stunt man or a big-shot producer with a cigar and a sports car. I don't reckon so. Because if he was, why's she at this school? Why's she even in Peckham? But McCardle's got his eye on her – on all of us – so I start thinking about me instead. Where I'm going.

"Dream big," that's what Otis says. But he says, "Don't forget where you come from" and all. He's big on mottos, Otis. Everything he says is like it's in some fancy font stuck on a picture of sunset on your Facebook feed. But I do it anyway. I dream big. I

37

dream I'm the Prime Minister, the youngest ever, and I make all these laws that say no one got to eat fish or wear ugly shoes but we all got to pick up litter and give homeless people sandwiches and adopt all the unwanted babies and stray dogs before anyone breeds any new ones. But not just that, in my plan I've written books too. This whole series about a girl who comes from Peckham and she looks like me or any of us, you know, nothing special, only she can see inside heads and knows what everyone's thinking all the time, so she becomes a detective and solves all these cold cases, locking up masterminds like Digits McPhee and Sugar Slim. Only this one mastermind, Fats Bojangles, kidnaps her and uses her to steal from his enemies, and I'm just working out how she's going to get away when McCardle tells us time's up.

"Who's going to tell us what the future holds then?" he asks.

No one puts their hand up. Like, duh.

"Come on, someone, or I'll lucky dip you. What about you?"

I look around to see who he's looking at, but the girl behind's looking straight back at me. And so's everyone else, including Angel.

"Go on, Ash," she says. "I dare you."

"Hey, hey. We're not playing games," says McCardle. "Just read. Go on, Asha, is it?"

I nod. And take a breath. And I read, ignoring the snickers and the catcalls and the *oh my god*s from the back row. When I'm done there's silence. For just one second. And McCardle's looking at me like he don't know whether to laugh or clap or send me up the Maudsley with the mentalists. I glance over at Angel but she's staring at him and all, like she's willing him to try it, just try it. Only I don't know what.

"See me after class," he says eventually. "Right, Bradley, it's your lucky day. You're up next."

Am I in trouble? I write on my notepad as Bradley tells us he's going to be the next Didier Drogba, only white.

Angel pulls it over, reads it, snorts. Then writes

39

underneath in her purple gel pen: *No. He probably fancies you.*

Kelly grabs the pad. *Jealous?* she writes.

"As if, beeyatch," Angel whispers.

Only her face don't look *as if* at all. But I don't get the chance to write back because she's got McCardle's attention anyway and not in the way I reckon she wants it.

"Angel, that's your last warning."

"It wasn't just me," she says and slumps back in her chair.

And she's right. It wasn't. "Sorry," I volunteer.

McCardle looks at me, and nods. "All right. Respec' for Bradley here, huh? Even if he does support Chelsea."

Angel elbows me to pass the pad, like she's got something more she wants to say and it's all about McCardle. But I don't want to know what it is, not 'til I know what he got to say to me. So I pull it down onto my lap and I don't write anything else. I just wait to find out what I've done.

Four

The bell rings and chaos reigns. There's no filing out like at Queen Mary's, here it's insults being hurled and screwed-up bits of paper being thrown and mobiles being pulled out of back pockets and bags.

"Shall I meet you in the playground?" asks Patience as she passes.

But Angel pushes in.

"'Playground'? This isn't primary, *Patience*." She spits the word out like it's anything but. Turns to me. "We'll wait for you outside, yeah?"

41

"OK," I say, like it's nothing. "Ta."

"Don't let him do nothing, either," she adds, loud enough for McCardle to hear. "You can have him if he tries anything."

McCardle shakes his head, smiling. "We're all in the gutter," he says. "And some of us are looking at the stars. But some of us can only see broken bottles and fag ends."

"Charming," Angel says. Only she's not charmed at all.

"Freak," adds Kelly, in full voice, as the door slams behind them.

McCardle's still shaking his head as he turns to me. "Friends of yours?"

"Maybe," I reply.

He pauses. "Look, I don't know you yet. But I get the feeling from your reports ... from what you wrote, those girls don't seem like they'd be your type."

"You sound like my mum," I say.

He laughs. "That not a good thing?"

I shake my head. "Nah. Not usually."

"You want to be a writer then?"

"Maybe."

"But in your piece—"

"I want to be lots of things, innit. But yeah, a writer. Like J.K. Rowling, maybe. You know how much she earns?" I ask him. "Five pounds a second. So that's, like, a hundred pounds just in the time we've been stood here. A hundred and five now."

"That what matters to you, is it? Money?" He seems disappointed. Like he's got Angel in front of him now, not me. And somehow I get how she feels, because I want to fix it, want him to think good of me. Only I don't act up, I do what he wants, say what he wants to hear.

"No," I reply quickly. Then, quieter, "Money don't mean nothing. Not really. It's . . . it's about being, I don't know, just someone. Someone who matters."

He nods. Like he gets it. "We should get on with it then," he says. "You're wasting valuable writing minutes."

43

I shrug, as he gets to the point.

"Listen, I thought you'd like to join my writing group. There's about ten of us so far. All years. Two others in yours – Patience and Kelley."

"Kelly Dooley?" I ask, like he's said "Father Christmas" or "Jesus" or "Taylor Swift".

"Kelley Eckersley," he replies. "Different spelling. It's Wednesday after school for a couple of hours. I bring biscuits and you bring your ideas and we just see what happens, you know."

I nod, only I don't know at all.

"You'd enjoy it. And it'd be good for you."

"Like broccoli?" I say.

"Nah, nicer than that. Fun too. Like broccoli dipped in chocolate."

"That don't sound that good," I say.

He laughs. "Maybe you're right. Maybe you can think of a better way to put it by Wednesday, huh?"

He's waiting for an answer. And I can tell he's not expecting it to be a "no".

But I don't give him a "yes" either. Not yet. "Wednesday?" I say.

"Room B14, end of the corridor."

I nod. "B14."

He opens the door for me to go. But as I step into the corridor, three words follow me out. "Stay gold, Ponyboy," he says.

I turn back. "Who's Ponyboy?" I ask.

"Seriously? You don't know?"

I shrug.

"We'll have to do something about that then," he says. "Wednesday, yeah."

"Wednesday," I repeat.

"You'll enjoy it," he says. "I promise."

"Like chocolate-coated broccoli," I say.

"Touché," he says, making like he's been stabbed. "Touché."

Angel and Kelly are in the corridor, backs against the wall.

"So what did 'e want then?" Angel asks. She's

45

texting as she says this, her eyes on her fingers, making out she don't care about the answer, I reckon. Only she does, I know it. So I play it down.

"Nothing. Writing group or something. After school. Don't know if I'll do it anyway," I lie.

"Whatever," she says, only I can tell it's anything but. "Sounds boring to me."

"Probably."

"Stupid cow." She switches the phone off, looks up. "Sorry, not you. My mum, innit. Only gone and invited Fat Brian over."

"Is he your . . . step-dad?" I ask.

Kelly laughs, her mouth open so I can see she's got another wodge of pink gum in there already.

"No chance," Angel says. "He's married to Mrs Fat Brian. Not that that puts my mum off. Can we go round yours, Kel? Who's in?"

Kelly shrugs. "Everyone, no one. How should I know. I only live there."

But that passes as a yes, and they don't even ask if I want to come, just take it as a done thing, like, duh, as if I'd say no. And then McCardle and Ponyboy are forgotten as my heart skips like I've won the lottery and I don't even care that the prize is a terrace on Ephraim Street with half a car in the front garden and three kids in the front room – two in nappies and one who definitely should be. It smells of dog and cigarettes, but I don't let on, 'cause it don't matter when something about the place still sparkles.

"That's Liam and Jake," Kelly says, nodding to the kids in nappies. "And this . . ." she swings the naked one up on her shoulders, "is Cheryl, ain't you."

The girl squeals and I smile, even though I'm thinking that kid could pee at any minute.

"Jesus, Kel, will you put her down."

I turn and see a woman standing there, like someone's clapped a magnifier on Kelly, or pumped her full of air, 'cause she's the spit of her, only eight stone heavier, and double that years older.

"All right, Mrs Dooley," Angel says. As if it could be anyone else.

"Where's Sharon?" asks Kelly, lowering a still-squealing Cheryl to the ground.

"Tea round her nan's," her mum says. "Who's this?" She nods at me.

"Asha," says Kelly. "She's new."

"Hello," I say. "Nice to meet you."

"Blimey." Mrs Dooley laughs. "Not from round here, then."

Angel sticks one hand on her hip. "Yeah, she is," she says, her eyes on mine. "Just sometimes she forgets."

"Don't blame her," says Mrs Dooley. "Go on up, before your sister gets back and turns your room into a karaoke. I'll bring you up something."

"Ah, thanks, Mam," Kelly says, all soft now, not like the way she spoke about her in English. "Can we 'ave Cokes, and Twixes?"

"No Twixes, Liam had the last. I've got Mars or Snickers."

"Mars," says Kelly.

"Angel?"

"Nothing ta. Diet, innit."

"Ah, get away. You're all skin and bone, girly."

"Thanks," Angel says, like she got an A on her exam.

Mrs Dooley looks at me. "Er, Snickers, thanks," I say.

"Good on you, girl." And somehow I feel like I got an A too.

Kelly's room is pink. The walls are pink. The carpet's pink. The curtains are pink. I feel like I've climbed into a wodge of bubblegum. Or someone's insides. We cram ourselves onto the bottom bunk bed, backs against the wall, legs stretched out over the duvet. Even that's pink.

"I can't eat Snickers, anyway," Angel says, eyeing me as I take the top layer of chocolate with my teeth. "Allergic to peanuts, innit."

"Bull," says Kelly. "I seen you eat Reese's Pieces when your dad sent 'em over that time."

Angel looks like she's been slapped, but she

49

pulls it back, shrugs it off. "That was ages ago."

"You can get them down Crackerjack anyway. I seen 'em. No point sending 'em over in the first place," Kelly adds.

"Whatever. Are we really gonna talk about peanuts all afternoon?" Angel says.

"Is your dad actually in Hollywood?" I ask.

"Yeah. What, you think I'm lying and all?" Angel snaps.

"No, I just meant, that's pretty cool, innit," I say quickly.

Angel shrugs. "He lives in this condo – that means flat – with my step-monster, Cindy."

"She's a stripper," adds Kelly.

"For real?" I blurt out.

"No, in a film." Angel rolls her eyes. "Yes, for real. Sad, innit. But he sends me stuff. Like this."

She reaches down her shirt and pulls out a silver necklace with a Tiffany heart on the end. I know that's what it is 'cause Mum's got one. Ellis gave it to her last Christmas. Four weeks before he left her.

Left me. Only I don't want to think about him, not right now.

"I didn't think you were allowed to wear jewellery to school," I say. Then regret it.

"What, and you do everything you're told, do you?" snaps Angel.

I think about where I am, and who I'm with. "No," I say. "I wish my dad was in Hollywood," I add quickly.

"With a stripper?" asks Kelly.

I shrug. Maybe he is with a stripper. I don't know. I don't care. Then I remember something, feel a shiver in me. "What's your dad do, Kelly?" I ask.

Kelly eyes me. "What doesn't he do?" she says, and laughs.

But that's not what I meant. "He ... he still about?" I ask.

"Sometimes," she says. "He's away at the moment."

I feel my stomach turn, like I can smell sour milk.

"Newcastle, innit, Kel?" says Angel. "He's with Ronan's dad, building some stadium or something."

51

The milk drains away. "Who's Ronan?" I ask.

"One of my cousins," says Kelly. "What Angel's got the hots for."

"Oh my god, I haven't," says Angel, throwing a cushion at Kelly.

"Ronan and Angel up a tree..." sings Kelly, throwing it back.

"Seriously, shut up," says Angel.

"Oh come on, you went to second base with him at Stacey Woodley's thirteenth," Kelly protests.

"We was just fooling around," says Angel. "I don't love him or nothing." She changes the subject from her to me. "What about you? You been to second?"

I know what second base is. I read it in a magazine. First base is kissing, second is them touching your boobs, third is touching down there and fourth base is doing it. I only been to first. And only with Joe. And only that one time.

"That's for me to know and you to find out," I sing-song, like I'm speaking my lines in a show on telly.

"Tease," says Kelly.

Angel eyes me. "You got a boyfriend then?"

I think about Joe. And about that other boy I conjured up yesterday out of magazine photos and movie scripts. And neither of them fit that description.

"I told you," I say. "We got broken up, innit."

"If I loved someone, I wouldn't let anyone break us up," says Angel. "I'd run off with them."

"What, like Ronan?" says Kelly. "Or McCardle?"

Angel turns. "Piss off," she snaps. "Anyway, you know what I mean." She turns to me again. "So no one since then?"

She arches one perfect eyebrow and I think of mine, too thick. Only Mum won't let me pluck them, not yet. Says I'm too young. Then I get an idea, to get off the subject and get me what I want.

"Will you do my eyebrows?" I ask. "You know, pluck them." Because I can say it's in sympathy with Mum, innit. Or just say "whatever" because it's not like she can do much from where she's lying. Not now Ellis is gone and Otis don't care about eyebrows big or small, he say all that matters is "heart and head, chile". Only he don't go to secondary school where all that matters is hair and getting rid of it everywhere except on your head. That and how big your boobs are and which base you've been to.

"Makeover!" cries Kelly, like she's got a full house down the bingo hall.

"Oh my god. Totally," says Angel. "Shit. I wish we were at mine. We got better stuff there. No offence."

"None taken," says Kelly. "We can't all have mums who work up Debenhams' make-up counter, innit. Mine'd be lucky to get a job down Superdrug."

"Your mum's all right," I say, thinking of the way she let me in, gave us all drinks and stuff, let us up here. Mine wouldn't have done that. Otis, maybe. But he'd have kept us all in the front room, asking us questions and feeding us seed cake and stories of the old days.

Kelly shrugs. "S'pose. She ain't no model though. Or a lawyer. Is it like on telly?"

"What?" I ask.

"You know. Does she wear a wig and that?"

I think of Mum on the sofa: her head bald like a black egg; the wig she got on the NHS on a stand in bathroom. I know that's not the kind Kelly means, but it's still not a lie.

"Yeah, sometimes," I say.

"We should wait," says Angel, then. "Do the makeover another day when Fat Brian's not about and my mum's out. Saturday maybe. Then we can put your makeover to use, innit. Go up Westfield or something."

"Why wait 'til then?" asks Kelly.

Angel pauses, looks at her, then straight at me. I see it in her eyes then, in the way they narrow. Plotting, planning, dreaming.

"Truth or dare," she says to me.

"What?" I ask.

"Pick one."

"Yeah," says Kelly. "Truth or dare. If you want to hang around with us, you got to play, innit."

"Last month I dared Kelly to climb the wall of one of the houses up Dulwich and she done it," Angel says.

"And I nicked a gnome and all," adds Kelly. "Angel's boring. She always picks truth. Only half the time I reckon she's lying anyway."

"Piss off. I never lied about going to second with Ronan. Or about the time Fergus Fletcher touched my boob behind Iceland. And I done dares. What about when I went to church 'cause you dared me and I laughed so hard I was nearly sick in that bowl thing?"

"Font," says Kelly. "And chill, yeah? Come on, Ash, which is it?"

And it's so obvious. Because what's the point in picking truth? Angel knows it – the truth's one big disappointment so why would you tell it? But a dare, a dare is bright lights and red carpet and the flash of cameras. It's possibility and chance and luck, good or bad. A dare means things can change. And who wouldn't want that?

"Dare," I say. "I pick dare."

Angel smiles, like now she got the cream. "I dare you to bunk off with us on Friday and come round mine."

And I don't skip a beat when I say, "Done."

It's not 'til I get home that I feel the comedown. 'Til I see Otis peeling carrots and potatoes for stew and whistling along to the radio and he gives me a smile and says, "All right, chile?" and I nod. 'Til I see my mum watching some game show I know she hates, just like she hates all game shows and soaps and anything on BBC3. But the remote's too far for her to reach and I know she don't want to ask Otis while he's cooking. I flick the channel onto the news.

"Thank you, Asha," she says.

"*De nada*," I say.

I lie in my bed in the box room that night, Otis snoring on the other side of the wall, Mum in the front room, the telly still going 'cause the chemo means she can't sleep, just like she can't eat dinner no matter how many times Otis tries to coax her. I got my headphones on to drown it all out – the noise, this flat, this life she's living, she wants me to live – and I weigh up my choice like it's between red socks or blue. The dare, against being found out. Against what would happen: that I'd prove her right about this school, about the girls, that they're all trouble.

Only why's she so sure that I'm not? Why am I different, better? 'Cause I'm like her?

I don't want to be. I don't want to be anything like her. Not one cell of me. Not like my dad, neither. I'm a new kind of girl. Made of books and films and lines from this song that's playing – all the best bits. I can do it all. I can write the stories like McCardle wants. Be that girl who gets an A. But I can do other things too. I can pluck my eyebrows. I can go to second base. I can do anything I want if I put my mind to it. Just like she says.

So, yes, I can dare.

And I feel it then, like I felt it round Kelly's. The

power in that one little word is vast, bigger than the Grand Canyon or Everest or a trip to the moon. It's so strong and I feel it push me down the big dipper, feel it put its hand hard against the waltzer and spin me 'til I'm whirling. "Scream if you want to go faster!" it shouts above the clanging of the music.

And inside I let out a whoop.

Five

When you're flying, when you're so high you think you can touch stars or satellites or at least the wing of a parakeet, there's always someone to pull you back down to earth. Only for once it's not Otis, or Mum, or Patience with her *I wouldn't do that if I were you*s. It's not even Joe 'cause I'm sure as sugar not telling him what I'm up to, 'cause I know he'd get all pale and sweaty and tell me not to. No, the sand in my shoe is McCardle.

Writing group's going like a dream. Like a

honey-coated peanut, I tell him, because that's protein and sugar, so it's sort of good for you and it tastes good, whatever Angel says. And he's grinning his big gold-toothed smile and calling me J.K., and Kelley Eckersley offers me a custard cream and then we're all working together, writing a poem about what Peckham would look like if we'd come from another planet, which isn't all that hard for me.

But then, at the end, when I'm helping him stack the chairs so the cleaner can come in, he pulls something out his back pocket and hands it to me.

"Here," he says.

"What's this?" I ask, like I'm the class dunce, 'cause I can see exactly what it is. It's a book. Only not just any book. This one's old, cover torn at one corner, pages yellowed, spine broken where it's been bent back for easy reading. This book's been read and not just once, a hundred times maybe. This book's loved.

And he's giving it to me.

"*The Outsiders*," I read. Then I look at the picture – a bunch of cowboys, it looks like, with slicked-back quiffs, fighting on their minds and fags in their mouths. "Isn't it . . . for boys?" I ask.

McCardle shrugs. "Books are for whoever wants them," he says. "Whoever they speak to. This one spoke to me, and I reckon maybe it will to you. Besides, it's written by a woman."

"S.E. Hinton?" I read.

"Susan," he says. "Like J.K. is Joanne really. Like you'd be . . ."

"A.J.," I say. "A.J. Wright."

He smiles. "Don't sound half bad, does it."

"I guess not," I say. 'Cause it don't. It don't at all. "When d'you want it back?"

"Whenever," he says. "When you're done. Just look after it, yeah? That book's been a long way with me. Seen me through some tough times. More precious than gold, those pages are. Worth more to me than all the riches in the kingdom, more than Arsenal winning the double."

I laugh then, 'cause it's meant to be funny, but I know he ain't joking. "I will."

"Good," he says with a nod. "If you've started by then, you can let me know what you think on Friday."

I don't know what he means for a moment. "Friday?"

"English? Second period. Unless you got something better to do?"

My stomach flips and I have to stick my hands behind my back so he won't see them shake. "I'll be there," I say.

But I won't. I'll be with Angel.

She's outside the gates. I didn't ask her to wait or to come back, but something's on her mind 'cause she's there anyway.

"Want to get a Coke?" she says.

I nod. "Quick though, I got to be back by five."

She rolls her eyes. "What, or the bears'll get you?"

"Something like that."

63

"Fine, just walk with me to Maccy D's, yeah? Mum's not back and I'm starving."

I nod and we fall in line, our shoes hitting the same slow stride, hers patent-leather-tipped, mine matt, the pale grey of pleather underneath showing through the plastic coating. But she don't care, or don't seem to right now. She got other things on her mind.

"So what was it like, then? Bet it was like detention."

I don't want to disappoint her. But I don't want to diss McCardle either. Not when he's trusted me with treasure. My hand goes automatically to my pocket, protecting what's inside.

"It was all right," I say. "We had biscuits."

"Oh, well, must've been a right party, then." She says it all sarky-like. Sassy, even. But you got to read between the lines, that's what the magazines say. 'Cause someone might be saying, "I hate you, you're a right tosser," when what they really mean is, "I love you".

"You could come," I say.

"Yeah, right," she says. "Like he'd let me."

"I could ask him. If you like."

"Yeah, well I don't like."

She's quiet then, only I can feel the thinking, and feel something else and all – her eyes on me. I twist my head quick, catch her staring, her top lip clamped between her teeth. "What?" I ask.

"What's in your pocket?" she says. "You keep touching it like you nicked something."

And you'd know all about that, I think. Only instead of feeling shame for her, I get that thrill again. That fairground jolt of possibility. Then the quick pull-up when I realise I'm going to disappoint her.

"Nothing," I say. "Just a book."

But for some reason a book's more interesting right now than a robbed phone 'cause she reaches over and pulls it out like it's a rabbit out of a hat.

"*The Outsiders*," she reads. "Where'd you get that?"

"Just … McCardle," I admit. "He lent it."

She stops dead then, sending a woman with a buggy swerving round us, tutting.

"Cow," says Angel. But she's not looking up; all she can see's the book.

She opens the front cover, clocks something I hadn't noticed, three words in neat black biro. *Stay gold, Ponyboy*, it says. Then a signature – *T. Lutter* – the L and the Ts all loops, like there's all the ink in the world and he, or she, is worth it.

"Who the eff's Ponyboy?" she asks.

Who the eff's T. Lutter? I think. "I don't know," I say.

Angel snaps the book shut, holds out it. "Here," she says.

Only when I go to take it, she drops it on the floor.

"Oops, butterfingers." And she's laughing like it's not the oldest, crappest joke in the world.

"Careful," I say, snatching it up and checking for dirt, or worse.

"It's just a book, Ash," she says. "Keep your wig on."

"I know," I say. "Just a book." Only I push it back down in my pocket, where it's safe. 'Cause I'm pretty sure it's not just any book.

I'm right and all. I know that soon as I start it in bed that night.

It's set ages ago, in the 1960s, and in America. And it's about these two gangs: the Greasers, the poor kids who got greased-back hair and attitude, and the Socs – which is short for Society – they're the rich ones, the ones with flash cars and futures. They got names too, good ones – Dallas and Two-Bit and Sodapop and Johnnycake. And Ponyboy. He's in it. Not just in it – he wrote it. Or it's supposed to sound like that, 'cause it's all in his voice, only it's really that S.E. Hinton woman – girl even. 'Cause when I read the blurb on the back I find out that she was only seventeen when she wrote it. Just a kid, really, not much older than me.

67

Maybe I'll do that, I think. Write a book when I'm seventeen.

Only I got to do some living first, I reckon, like she did. Got to have a story to write down. And that's where Angel comes in.

Six

I've done dares before. I've climbed trees on the Rye so tall you that when you look down dogs are small as ants, and the sound of your mum shouting at you to get down is lost on the wind. I've worn fancy dress down Epping High Road on a Saturday, a furry tiger drinking pink milk through a straw. I've swallowed a beetle once, a dead one, 'cause some girl called Flick bet me I wouldn't.

But this dare's the biggest.

We got it sussed though. Got ourselves a plan, like

on *Charlie's Angels*, 'cause that's who I said we were, and Kelly, she liked that, 'cause no one ever called her an angel before. We're going to email the school on our mums' accounts. Say we all got food poisoning round Kelly's last night. She says it won't be the first time 'cause her mam's always getting knock-off sausages off the meat man in the pub, so they'll totally believe us.

I feel sick when I do it. My fingers sweaty and slipping off the keys, the *what-ifs* dancing around in front of me, blurring the words on the screen: *What if she walks in right now and catches me? What if school emails back and she hears the ping and I'm done for?*

But I got replies and all: I can delete anything school sends back, though Angel says they never bother 'cause Miss Merritt, she's the secretary, is too busy doing her nails and eyeing up Mr Anthony who does PE to give a toss about stuff like that. Besides, Mum don't go near her phone or computer at the moment, in case it's Ellis or her old work. She says she don't need their pity, she needs their money and if they're not going to pay her they can leave well alone. Otis, he's out on shift and I got Patience covered and all. I'm going to leave early so she'll think I've gone already, then I'll text her later to tell her I'm ill, innit, and I'll get my homework off her tomorrow. And it's not really lying, I tell myself. It's just a story. All stories are lies if you think about it, and where would we be without them? Anyway, she's got Dennis to sit with, and the grinning girls. They can bother God together, innit.

The plan's golden. Except for McCardle. When I let him into my head it's like a dent, or a spot of mould growing. So I push him out again, him and Ponyboy. For now, anyway. 'Cause that's a book, and this is real life and for once, it's going to be better than words.

It's weird walking down Rye Lane with all those other kids in uniforms when you know they've got six slow hours of whiteboards and writing and jostling down corridors in front of them, and you've got a flash flat and freedom. Angel texted me the address and I sucked my teeth when I read it, 'cause it's the new building next to the surgery – all glass walls and balconies and city boys. The kind Otis says is pushing the good folk out of Peckham.

"Why you want a balcony to look at buses and breathe exhaust?" he says every time we go past.

Mum don't say nothing 'cause she had her eye on them flats 'til we went up Epping. Joe don't say nothing either but I know he's thinking it would be the best flat on earth if he could watch buses all day. For once I'm with Mum and Joe, 'cause I reckon I wouldn't mind Angel's flat at all.

It's like in one of those magazines you get at the dentist's, or on *DIY SOS*, only the *after* bit. Kelly's is the *before* – all dirty paint and broken banisters and toys where there shouldn't be none. This place though, this shines. It's kind of like our old house in Epping – sharp and clean and smelling of lemon – only as if someone dunked that in glue and threw up glitter all over it, plus a whole album of pictures of

Angel and her mum. They're everywhere: Angel and her mum in a field, all soft focus like you're looking at them through Vaseline. A primary-school Angel with eyeshadow on even though she's only seven or eight. Angel's mum on a fur rug with too much boob showing. I don't ever want to see my mum like that. Not that she's got much to show now, anyway.

Kelly's already on the sofa when I get there, eating a bag of Minstrels. She's always eating junk, only she's as skinny as a stick. It's like inside her there's this giant tapeworm that's swallowing the food up again. That can happen, I saw it on telly.

"Here, Ash." She throws me one and I try to catch it in my mouth, only it misses and falls on the glass coffee table.

"Watch it," says Angel, plopping down on the sofa next to Kelly. "She'll go mental if we drop stuff, innit."

I pick the chocolate up quick and flick it in my mouth. *Breakfast of champions*, I think, only I don't say it 'cause it's something I read in a book and they might think I'm mental.

"Take your shoes off and all," adds Angel. "She's totally OCD. Once she hoovered the balcony. I'm not even joking. It's amazing she even lets Fat Brian in 'cause he sweats like a pig and she has to change the sheets every time he's been."

"That is minging," laughs Kelly, shaking her head.

"Tell me about it."

Angel eyes me as I pull my school shoes off and sit down on the La-Z-Boy. "Your mum got a boyfriend?"

"Not any more," I say, pulling the lever so the foot-rest slams up into place, only I do it too hard and the whole thing tips back at the same time.

"Shit," I say.

Angel laughs as I pull the lever again, right myself, my cheeks burning.

"So, did she dump him or did he dump her?" she asks. "Mum dumps all hers in the end. None of 'em last, 'cause they all cheat or steal or turn out to be as boring as they look. I'm amazed Fat Brian's lasted."

"Only 'cause his wallet's as big as his arse," says Kelly, and we all laugh and me the loudest, 'cause then I don't have to talk about Ellis walking out and leaving us broke. I don't even like thinking about it – getting home from school that day and his bags are sat in the hallway and Mum's shut in her room. I said he was a loser, a chicken and that I hated him for what he was doing. Not that I liked him all that much to start with. Only I didn't say it out loud 'cause he never gave me the chance. Just came home from work, put the suitcases in the back of his shitty Fiat and drove off towards Harlow.

I change the subject. "I saw this thing on the news once," I start. "This bloke up North – in Bradford or Leeds or somewhere – he was keeping monkeys. He was going to breed himself an army of them and take over the world. Only the neighbours reported him for the smell and when the police came they were all sitting on the sofa watching *Deal or No Deal* and

75

eating pizza. My mum says that's the trouble with men. Never live up to their promise."

Angel's laughing so much she's crying now and Kelly's spat some chocolate down her shirt.

"You're funny, Ash," says Angel.

"Funny looking," says Kelly.

"Ha ha," I say, 'cause I know she means it as a joke.

"We should do those eyebrows though," says Angel.

"And outfit," adds Kelly. "And hair and make-up and nails. You can be our guinea pig."

"Model!" Angel elbows her.

"Whatever," says Kelly. "Bags I get the left one."

It must be weird, being a beautician. Staring at people's faces close up like that – all the spots and scars and strange bits. Smelling what they had for breakfast; knowing they can smell you and all. Angel's so covered in Impulse I can't tell about what she ate, but I can see the dark spot in the blue of her right eye, see the pale fuzz of hair on her cheek like a peach.

She pulls.

"Ow. God." I smack my hand over my eye for the fifth time. "You do know what you're doing, don't you?"

She leans back, hand on her hip. "Are you doubting me?" she asks. "I learned from the master, innit."

"What, Zoella?" I ask.

Kel snorts. "No, her mum, innit."

"Now shut up and keep still, or you're gonna end up looking like that girl in Year Eleven – what's she called?"

"What, Jade Priestly?" asks Kel.

"That's her. She reckoned she got 'em done up West by a 'brow artist', only whoever done it must be crap at art 'cause one's, like, way higher than the other."

I don't move after that, I just sit, silent like, hands under my backside, fingers crossed. They do my make-up and all only they don't let me look in the mirror 'til they're done, just like on telly. So I can have that moment, like the ugly duckling when it sees itself turned into the swan.

Only when I look, I'm not a swan, not even a black one. I'm more like a flamingo, or a peacock, or some tropical bird they haven't discovered yet with feathers on their eyelids and pink and green shimmering all over their face. My eyebrows have shrunk to a narrow line. One's a bit thinner than the other – the one that hurt more, the one that Kelly did. I got fake eyelashes and all so my eyes stand out like they're ogling the wonders of the world. And the clothes Angel lent me – a mini-skirt and a boob tube; two tight hoops of green lycra – show every bump and bone.

I look weird. But I look good too.

"Let's get this party started," says Angel and dances across the room. She turns up the volume on the iPod dock and Rihanna's belting it out, singing about her umbrella and me and Kel and Angel we're dancing like no one's watching.

"You know what we should do," says Kel. "Cocktails!"

"Like virgin ones?" I ask, 'cause I had one of those once at Mum's work Christmas party. A strawberry mocktail with a sparkler in it. Like sticking a firework on a smoothie really, if you think about it.

"Grow up," says Angel.

She opens this cupboard and inside are rows of bottles, some full, some half-empty but I don't know of what.

"How about a Cosmo?" Angel pulls a bottle out and dangles it.

"Nice one," says Kelly.

"Ash?"

I see a white bottle at the back, one I recognise 'cause Otis got one for when Mrs Joyful King come over. "I'll have a Malibu," I say. Then I remember something I heard on *Eastenders*. "Straight."

"Classy," says Angel and pours it into a shot glass for me.

"Cheers," says Kelly.

"Cheers," we echo.

They start sipping theirs but I just sniff mine. It smells of car freshener and I know I'm not going to drink it without chucking up.

"Come on," says Angel. "This is a party, innit. Drink up."

I lift the glass and put the rim on my lips, but when she turns back to link arms with Kelly I pour it out into this vase that's on the windowsill. 'Cause the dare was just bunking. Getting drunk wasn't ever part of the deal.

Nor was smoking.

Angel and Kelly have had two Cosmos each and are lying on Angel's bed puffing Marlboro Light smoke out the window so her mum don't smell it later. Kelly says her mum won't notice and even if she does she'll think it was her anyway.

I say I don't want one, ta.

"I always fancy a fag after lunch," says Kelly. Even

though lunch was just a packet of pretzels and some Dairylea Dunkables.

"How come you don't smoke, then?" asks Angel.

"How come you do?" I want to ask. And I want to tell her all the facts I know. That every cigarette shortens your life by eleven minutes. That a hundred thousand people a year die of smoking just in England. That lung cancer is one of the worst ones you can get and I'm already worried I'm going to get the breast kind 'cause it runs in the family.

Mum's not the only one, see. Her mum died of it and all, the one that was married to Otis, when I was only four. And her aunts before her. Mum reckons I should get the test. They can do that, check to see if you're carrying the cancer gene. I said no, ta. There's nothing there to get cancer in anyway, not yet, not even in this boob tube.

"When you're older then," said Mum.

I said there'd be a cure by then.

"And we'll live on the moon and fly about with jet packs," she replied and I hadn't got anything to say to that. And I haven't got anything to say to Angel neither except for "'cause".

"Chicken," she says.

"Whatever," says I. And I watch MTV until it's half three and then I take off the clothes and the eyelashes and put my uniform back on and me and Kel walk along the High Road and back down Lyndhurst Way. She peels off down Ephraim and then it's just me. Or at least I think it is.

"Asha. Wait up!" I hear from behind me. I don't even need to turn round to know it's Patience.

"I thought you were sick," she pants as she catches up and walks alongside me. I look over and I can see she's sweating she's run so hard.

"I-I was," I say. "Only then I felt a bit better and was going to come into school last thing and get my work only I was sick again on the corner – this dog started eating it, I swear it was the grossest thing ever." I add that bit 'cause if you're going to lie you got to make it really long and add detail. I learned that off *Sherlock*.

"Here you go." She hands me a Morrison's bag with some papers inside.

"Just Spanish and English. McCardle was in a right mood so we've got a whole essay to do by Tuesday."

"Ta," I say, and smile at her.

She stares back.

"What?" I say, all defensive-like.

"You've got glitter on your face," she says. "And your eyebrows look weird."

"Thanks," I say, rubbing my cheeks and wishing I'd done a better job with the wipes.

She's quiet for a second then, putting two and two together. And I know she's in top group maths so she's bound to get the right answer.

"Were you really sick or were you round Angel's? Because her and Kelly weren't in English either."

"We were sick," I protest. "All of us. Dodgy pork, innit."

But Patience don't seem convinced, by our alibi or the eyebrows. And Otis isn't that impressed neither when I get home.

83

"Lord, chile, what you do to your face?"

"What is it, Otis?" My mum's voice comes from the living room.

"Brilliant," I say under my breath.

"Watch your mouth," says Otis. "And go show your mother. It for her to say something, not me."

I push open the door to the front room and staleness bursts out like a trapped sparrow.

"Show me," Mum says. So I do.

"Who did that to you?" she says after a minute.

"I did," I say, 'cause it's easier that way. "I borrowed this girl's tweezers off her at lunch and done it in the toilets."

"'Did it'," she corrects.

Whatever, I think.

"You look too old," she says finally. "Like a lamb dressed up as mutton. Go wash your face."

Once upon a time she'd have bawled me out. Told me I was bringing shame on myself. Would have marched me to the bathroom herself. But the fight's gone, or most of it. Or maybe she don't care, like it's taking all her energy to battle with her own body, and me? I'm a lost cause anyway.

But I do what she tells me. And I smile as I do it 'cause even though no one likes my eyebrows 'cept me and Angel and Kel, even though I didn't drink nothing or smoke nothing and they think I'm a sadcase 'cause of it, even though bunking off was kind of boring in the end, I did it. I did the dare, and I reckon I got away with it. And more than that, I'm one of them now. It's like the Greasers, I think – Ponyboy's gang in the book McCardle gave me. He's got Sodapop and Johnnycake and I got Angel and Kelly. They're family. Crew. They stick together, no matter what. And they matter, their names are known.

And the bell on the waltzer clangs again as the ride slows to a still-giddy halt.

Seven

Joe don't like the eyebrows.

"Why'd you do that, Ash?" he asks.

We're sitting on a bench in a park up Forest Hill, where he lives now. He said he'd come down the Rye only I thought we might bump into Angel and Kel and I didn't want to have to explain that one. Plus Angel's already got the hump 'cause her mum found the Malibu in the vase when she was having one of her OCD frenzies. She's not mad about the fact Angel was drinking so much as the mess, only like Angel says, she can't get too mad 'cause Angel could just text Mrs Fat Brian if she wanted – she got the number off his mobile one time for collateral – and that would be the end of that.

"Just because," I say. "Don't you like them?"

"It's not that," he says. "It's just different. You're different."

"I'm still me," I say. "Just better. Like version 2.0 or an iPhone upgrade, innit."

Joe shrugs. "S'pose."

He's quiet for a bit though, then. So I know he's lying.

"How's your mum?" he asks eventually.

"Well she's not risen like freaking Lazarus if that's what you mean."

He looks at me like I've slapped him. Maybe I have. Words hurt sometimes, more than sticks and stones, no matter what that rhyme says.

"Sorry," I say.

"S'OK," he replies quickly. Too quickly. Because

he should stand up for himself. Be a man, I think. Like Dallas or Ponyboy.

But he's not Ponyboy. He's not a Greaser. He's just Joe.

"Who's Lazarus?" he asks.

"Some dead bloke in the Bible," I say. "I know Mum ain't dead, but she lies on that sofa like she might as well be. And Ellis called last night and all so she's in a right mood now."

"What did he want?"

"Dunno. Otis answered the phone and Mum wouldn't talk to him. Probably left his shoes at the house. Or his balls. Too late anyway, everything's in storage down Catford and I can't see us getting it out again any time soon."

He got no answer to that so he changes the subject to something else I don't want to talk about. "School all right? Who d'you hang about with?"

"Mostly Patience," I reply. "One or two others are all right" is all I got to say on Angel and Kel, for now anyway. I'd rather talk about telly. About

Eastenders or *Corrie* or this thing I saw about space.

"Did you know that a day on Mars is twenty-four hours and thirty-seven minutes," I say. "It's amazing. It's almost the same as us."

And that's how it goes. We talk about nothing and everything, just like we used to. The way orange Smarties are the only ones with a flavour. The first time Joe ate anchovies and nearly threw up. The last episode of *Doctor Who*. Life, and television, and books, too. He tells me about Huck Finn for the bazillionth time and I tell him about Ponyboy and Sodapop, and the rumbles between the Greasers and the Socs.

"What's a rumble?" he says.

"A fight," I tell him. "Same as here. Just there's more of them. And more knives."

"But if Ponyboy knows it's wrong, why does he join in?" he asks.

"I don't know," I say. "Because sometimes being bad feels good?"

"Maybe," he says. "But only, say, eating three

89

vegetables a day instead of five. Not fighting with knives."

"Yeah," I say, "but he's part of a gang, innit. In gangs you stick together."

He's quiet then, for a bit. "Ponyboy should be careful," he says eventually.

"I know," I say. 'Cause I'm worried for Ponyboy too. And we're both quiet now. But not for long, soon we're back on why denim's called denim and how much footballers get paid and whether Bloater really used to be a woman or if that's just another dumb rumour like the one about Mrs Barlow who teaches DT being Gary Barlow's mum.

We say goodbye at the bus stop up the top of Lordship Lane.

"Have a good week at school," he says.

"Yeah, you too," I say.

And I feel a little jump in me then, like we gone over a hump too quick in the car.

'Cause school means I'll see Angel and Kel again, and that's a good thing.

But then I get another jerk, the bad kind. Because it means I'll see McCardle too.

He got a right bee in his bonnet. Mainly 'cause half of us haven't read the chapters we were supposed to. Not me, I read them all and more besides. Why wouldn't I? 'Cause books are just like films on paper, really. You still get lost in them. Still get to be someone else more exciting for a bit. If I was someone in a book I'd be Heidi maybe, living up a mountain with my grandpa. Or Hermione, doing all them spells and beating the boys at it. Or Cherry Valance in *The Outsiders*, I think. All red hair and her own car and looks that boys fight over. Or anyone, anyone but me stuck here listen to McCardle arguing with Kel.

"I tried watching the film, sir," she says. "But our internet was down 'cause Liam peed on the router, not even joking. We thought he was going to be electrocuted only the light just went off."

"You've got a copy of the book, haven't you? Why

do you lot rely on the internet for everything? Like it's the Oracle of Delphi. Like it's going to deliver you up your GCSEs on a silver platter. There's nothing you can learn online that you can't learn from books, you know."

I don't reckon that's true. I've learned loads off YouTube. Like how to do a fishtail plait and make a bomb. Not that I've done either. My hair's not long enough and what would I blow up anyway? But I don't argue, 'cause McCardle's already given me funny looks twice and when the bell rings he asks me to stay again, and I know it's not to talk about J.K. Rowling this time 'cause he closes the door and sits down on his desk, looking at me like he's working out if I'm the hero or the villain or the story.

"You were off Friday," he says.

And the lies start pouring out like they're no more than water from a jug. "I know, sir. I was ill, innit. Food poisoning."

"Kelly Dooley and Angel Jones were off as well."

"Same thing. We all had these sausages round Kelly's and the next thing you know we're all heaving into the toilet taking turns and everything. It was gross. Have you seen *Stand by Me* where this kid eats too many pies and there's a barf-o-rama?"

McCardle shakes his head.

"Well it was like that, anyway."

"You got sick that quick?" he says. "Strange. It usually takes a few hours at least."

"They were really minging, sir, those sausages. Seriously. Angel said she might as well have eaten a dog turd."

He's quiet for a bit then. Still checking me out.

"I got high hopes for you, Asha," he says. "High expectations."

I feel a shiver then, that coldness.

"What about Angel and Kelly," I say. "Don't you have high hopes for them and all?"

"For everyone," he replies. "But I've seen what happens. Once you're all out of here. Some of us escape. Some . . ." he trails off.

And I think of Darry then, Ponyboy's big brother, who should have gone to college, been a Soc, only the gang and no money stopped him. And I wonder if that's what happened to McCardle, or if it's worse.

"I started reading it," I say. "The book, I mean."

He smiles then, wide enough to see gold. "That's good," he says. "And?"

"I like it," I say. "Only I don't get why they don't all just stop fighting and talk about it instead and then no one would get hurt."

"I ask myself the same question many a time," he says. "But then there'd be no story."

"I suppose," I say.

"You got talent," he says. "Don't waste it. Don't take it for granted. Use it. Show up to class. To writing group. Speak up, too. You always got something to say but today the cat got your tongue."

"Still a bit ill, maybe," I lie, but this time it don't slip out so easy.

"All right," he says. "But listen to what I said,

yeah? Stay out of trouble. It's hard, I know. Trouble has a habit of finding us. But try, yeah?"

I nod. "I will," I say. "I'll try."

Only trying's not the same as doing, is it. And I can try all I want but I'm not even hiding from Trouble, I'm hanging out with it. I'm going to Trouble's house after school, sharing crisps with Trouble, bunking off with it.

And the trouble is, I like it.

Eight

But I do what he says – McCardle, I mean. I show up to class and writing group, and I speak up and all.

I put my hand up when he asks what *Frankenstein*'s about and not to say "zombies" like Bradley. I say it's about prejudice and justice and he nods and we talk about judging people by what they do, not what they look like, and I feel bad about judging Darryl Benson even though McCardle don't mention smell.

I write a story about a woman who keeps her dead husband's ashes in her kitchen cupboard 'cause she reckons he still talks to her. Only not in an urn 'cause it got broken by the son who was raging about how mean his dad was and how he never left him his fortune, so they're in an Alpen packet 'cause she figures he'll never look in there. Then one day the son comes home drunk and he's hungry and he eats his own dad, and he starts to talk like him and be nice like him so everyone's happy. Except for Patience who said it was disgusting.

I don't cheek nobody. I text Mum to say if I'm going to be late from school. I help Otis make tea, peeling stuff and chopping it, not moaning once my fingers are cold from the water or smell of onions.

I read the rest of *The Outsiders* and I feel sick when Ponyboy nearly drowns, and I smile when they save the children from the burning church, and cry when Ponyboy gets the copy of *Gone With the Wind*. And I meet Joe up the Rye and tell him the story too, 'cause he's been dying to find out and I promise I'll lend him a copy one day, only not this one, 'cause this one's too precious. And I got to give it back, only not yet, not 'til I read it all again and it's printed on my memory.

"You want to hear something I wrote?" I ask.

"Course," he says. "Tell me."

So I do, and he laughs and tells me I'm going to be famous one day, as famous as S.E. Hinton, and I say I won't forget him when I am. And he says "Promise?" and I say "Pinky-swear."

So, yeah, I stay out of trouble. I don't cross any lines, not even a toe.

Not until two weeks later when we're round Kel's after school watching *Deal or No Deal* and eating microwave pizza like those monkeys.

"Would you rather snog Noel Edmonds or Bloater?" asks Kel.

Angel makes like she's going to throw up. "That is totally disgusting, Kel."

"You got to pick one," Kel says. "That's the game."

"I'd rather die," says Angel. "I'd rather snog Darryl fricking Benson."

"Me too," I add. Though I think I'd rather die than snog him and all, whatever McCardle says about not judging people.

"Pick one," insists Kel. "Come on. What about when you did me and it was between Bloater and Seamus Rourke who's, like, my third cousin or something."

I know that name, I think. Then I see it, written out in blue gel pen, in Kelley Eckersley's handwriting. Her boyfriend, must be.

"It's not illegal to snog your own cousin," Angel says. "Not even your first one."

"It should be," says Kel. "Have you seen some of my cousins?"

"What about Ronan?" I tease. "I thought he was fit."

"Leaving him to Angel, innit," says Kel, feeding her crust to one of the dogs that're always under our feet, waiting for leftovers or a pat. "Anyway, it's not my turn. Pick one, Ang. No, wait. If you don't want those two, how about this: Ronan or McCardle?"

"How many times?" snaps Angel. "I don't fancy McCardle. I don't even like him. He's a right knob. Besides, he's only got eyes for Asha." She looks over at me with this smile that isn't.

"He hasn't," I say, quick. "Honest. We just like books, innit."

"Teacher's pet," Angel snorts, like that's worse.

"You wish," says Kel.

Angel shoots her a look that says *shut up* but I can see other stuff in it. Like maybe she does wish, but she's never going to let on. Not to us. "I'm bored of this game," she says instead. "I got a better one."

"What?" I ask.

Angel grins at me, and she got that look in her eyes again, like she's got magic in her, or menace. "Truth or dare," she says.

And that's when Trouble walks in. And I'm the one that opens the door for it and gives it a welcome. Because I know I shouldn't want to play. Should back off, like McCardle says. Be careful. Toe the line. Only those words – *truth or dare* – it's like someone lifted the lid off a big box of gold-wrapped chocolates and said, "Take your pick." They're too delicious to turn away from. Too full of sweetness, and possibility. The chance to be in a story so big it could be written down in black and white, or technicolour up on a big screen. And I can't say no to that, can I.

"You're on," I say.

"Again?" says Kel. "Aren't we too old for that?"

"Not me," says Angel. "Never. But if you'd rather go change some nappies or something be my guest."

"Fine," sighs Kel. "Angel, still your turn. Which d'you want?"

"Truth," says Angel.

"Oh, come on," says Kel. "You'll only make it up."

"As if," says Angel. "Was I lying when I said I fancied that guy in Burger King?"

"True," admits Kel. "Though it shouldn't be. Have you seen his tats?"

"I like a tattoo," Angel says. "It's like a mark of bravery, innit. Shows you're different."

"Not that different," says Kel. "Our Mick's got the same one of a swallow and he's not brave, he's an eejit. Must be or he wouldn't be inside."

I feel a flicker in my stomach. "Come on," I say. 'Cause I don't want to talk about her uncles or prison or even tattoos, I want to get on with the game.

"Right. Truth. Angel Jones, do you or do you not fancy McCardle?"

"Oh ha effing ha," she says. "Not."

"Liar," says Kel. "As usual. Anyway, my turn."

"Truth or dare," I say.

"Dare," she replies. "Obviously."

I got one. Been thinking about it for a week. Not as a dare, like. Just as something she should do. "I dare you to go to chess club."

Angel starts killing herself laughing. Kel elbows her one. "No. Fricking. WAY," she replies.

"I dared you, you got to. Besides, you'd be good at it. You're good at plans and stuff."

"Have you *seen* who's in chess club," says Kelly.

I shrug. "Chicken."

"I ain't chicken," she says. "I ain't scared of any of them. I just got higher standards, innit."

"So do it," says Angel, still smirking. "If you ain't scared."

Kel stares at me. If looks could kill I'd be six feet under. But then she smiles, and I know she's going to accept.

"All right," she says. "I'll do it. I'll show up. I'm not saying I'm going to play. But I'll show up."

"Don't forget to wear your anorak," says Angel.

"Whatever," says Kel. "Anyway, Asha's go. Truth or dare, Ash?"

"Dare," I say. 'Cause I'm not scared of chess club or maths club or even Ultimate flaming Frisbee. How d'you even know they're crap if you don't try? Besides, loads of celebrities play chess. Like Julia Roberts and Will Smith and the Pope. I read it in a magazine. Only then I think of something. What if it's not to join a club. I mean, I'm already in one, innit. What if it's something bigger. Something worse. And when I see Angel's mouth spread into a grin, I know it is.

"I got it," she says. "Let me do it."

Kel shrugs.

"I dare you . . ." she begins, drawing it out like it's the judgement on a TV talent show, "to snog . . . Seamus."

I think for a second, then remember what Kel just said. "What, Rourke?" I turn to her. "Your cousin?"

Kel nods, her tongue in her cheek like she's loving this.

"But . . . I thought he was going out with Kelley Eckersley," I say.

"Was," says Angel. "They split up, innit. She dumped him two days ago 'cause she heard off Stacey that he'd had his hand down Chelsea Bateman's top behind Maccy D's on Saturday night."

"Well he's not going to snog me if he's snogging Chelsea," I say.

"That wasn't anything," says Angel. "Just a hook-up."

"If it's even true," says Kel.

"What about Kelley, though," I say.

"What about her?" says Angel. "She's a stuck-up cow just 'cause she's in top set."

"And 'cause she got an extra E in her name," says Kelly. "She thinks it makes her all that."

She is all that, though. She's dead pretty, with this long hair like caramel, and she's clever and she's nice too, never groans at Dennis's sci-fi stories and she said my thing about the dead man in the Alpen packet was "genius". Why would I want to get on the wrong side of her?

"Anyway, it's not like you got a boyfriend, is it," says Angel. And it's not a question. So there's no answer to that.

"So, what?" I ask. "I'm supposed to just walk up to him and snog him in the corridor?"

"Don't be mental," says Kel. "We got to lay some groundwork first. I'll tell his sister Siobhan to tell him that you fancy him. Then we'll work out a time."

"So, deal?" asks Angel.

And I echo the contestant on the telly as I say the word. "Deal." And the audience claps and slaps me on the back. So hard they almost wind me.

Nine

I see Seamus at school the next day. I seen him before, but only the back of him when he was walking Kelley home once. And he walked all cocky. With a swagger, like all the boys in Year Nine do. But from the front, standing by the lockers arguing about who would win in a fight, Iron Man or Batman, he don't seem so full of it. He seems all right. He's not bad looking. Not boy band like Ronan is, with his blond hair all gelled back and his skinny jeans so tight I think they must be painful. But nice enough. His hair's dark. And his skin's pale, almost blue, like the thin skimmed milk Mum used to get before she stopped drinking it altogether. And Kel tells me he plays guitar and he once had a trial for Tottenham, which makes him sound like he's something, someone. Like he's more than meets the eye.

I mean, everyone's more than they look. Though you can work out a lot by clothes. I learned that from *Sherlock* and all. Like Mrs Joyful King. She got a cross round her neck on a chain so I know she's religious, and a locket as well so I know she got a man she loves or loved once upon a time. But they're silver not gold so she's not rich and neither is he. And her hair changes style every day so I know it's a wig, only she's always outside sweeping the doorstep so I know it ain't cancer like my mum. Not that Mum's ever worn the wig 'cause she only goes outside to go to the hospital and she just got a scarf for that.

Anyway, Seamus, I think maybe he's got a bigger story than that. Bigger than Joe's even. And on my way home I walk past McDonald's and I see this couple in the window, not even looking at each other. He's got his eye on his phone and she's just staring all sad at the litter outside and the pigeons. Like she thought she was getting a steak dinner and candles and violins and all that, and instead she got this. A Big Mac and some cold fries and a lump of a husband who don't even see her. And I think that could be me and Joe. In thirteen years, like McCardle said. And I don't want that. I want adventure and love – the big kind with arguments and Eiffel Towers and a wedding in *Hello*. And what if all that starts with snogging Seamus?

I feel bad for Kelley Eckersley though. On Wednesday I can tell she's still upset over her and him ending 'cause her eyes are red and she don't get hayfever, and when we have to write a love poem most people do Clinton Cards crap about lips like rosebuds but hers is all about a black heart and a dagger and other emo stuff.

On the way home I ask Patience if she's ever snogged anyone.

I can tell she's blushing even though her skin's way darker than mine. "Dennis held my hand," she says. "At Southend last Saturday. We were on the Ferris wheel and I was scared and he got my hand and held onto it the whole time and then he bought me a doughnut."

"That's nice," I say. But I think about those people in the window of Maccy D's again and I know I'm not going to be one of them.

And by the next day Kel's got it sorted anyway.

"Saturday," she says. "My dad's job's done and he's coming back from Newcastle so Mam's having a party, innit."

"How d'you know Seamus'll be there?" I ask. "Won't it just be grown-ups?"

She looks at me like I'm a moron. "He'll be there," she says. "They'll all be there. You'll see. Even Ronan."

But Angel's not listening. She's chanting, "Party,

party," and moving her hips like she's X-rated not 12A.

"Saturday," I say.

"I already texted Siobhan to tell her and she texted back to say she said your name at tea when their mam asked who else was going and she's almost definite that he nodded."

"He nodded?" I ask. 'Cause that don't sound like he likes me. That sounds like he could be chewing too hard or listening to the telly.

"It's a start," says Kel. "Besides, when Angel's done with you, he won't be able to resist."

I look at Angel with her skirt too short and her shirt too tight and the top button undone on purpose, and she's still dancing down on the tarmac, her hair swinging in the sun, and I think right then she looks like she might work magic.

"So, Saturday," I say. "You bringing anyone from chess club?"

'Cause she went in the end. Showed up Tuesday lunchtime and nearly made old Bloater choke on his chicken sandwich. I know 'cause me and Angel were watching outside through the window, so we could make sure she stayed and didn't just go in and pretend she forget a book or something and then leave and claim Bloater kicked her out. But she didn't and he didn't. And I was right, she was good, 'cause she beat this Year Seven called Lucas and next week's Bloater's going to let her play someone in her own year.

"Piss off," she says. But she's smiling so I wonder if she has got her eye on anyone from there after all, and I think people got it wrong. Grown-ups think doing dares is dumb, dangerous. But it's not, not when it can make you grin like Kel is right now.

"Laters, losers," says Angel as we reach the gate.

"See you," I say.

"Wouldn't want to be you," says Kel.

"Ha fricking ha," says Angel.

But I would. And on Saturday I'm going to be.

*

Angel wants to come over to mine before but I don't let her, do I. I'm not that daft. I tell her my mum won't let me out the house if I'm all dressed up, innit. And even though she can't have seen my mum since primary, she nods like she knows it's not a lie. Mum's the best excuse to keep them out even without the cancer.

"When am I going to see your house?" asks Angel. "What's in there, fricking snakes or something?"

"Something like that."

"I don't even know where you live."

"Yeah, you do," says Kel. "Lyndhurst, innit. I bet it's one of them big houses, three floors high."

"Maybe," I say. And that's not a lie either. I just don't tell her we only live on one of them floors, and only half of it at that.

So when I get my coat on Saturday night I'm dressed like I'm going to church group, which is exactly where I said I'd be.

"Don't be late," says Mum. "Eleven, you hear?"

"I hear," I say.

113

"And Mr Williams, he's going to walk you back?"

I nod. "You already asked me that."

Otis steps in. "Let her go, Chrissie, she be fine."

But Mum got this face on her like fine is the last thing I'll be.

"You know she worry," Otis says when he gets me on my own in the hallway. "And you know why."

I nod. I do. And I know what she's thinking. She's thinking that she met my dad when she was my age and he's the reason she dropped out of school and got pregnant when she should've been doing her A-levels.

"But I'm not like that, am I," I say to Otis.

He shakes his head. But in spite of his smile, he still got words of warning. "You better not be, girlie," he says.

By the time I leave Angel's I look like I might be, though. I'm in a gold dress that only comes down an inch below my bum and my hair's gelled right back and I got bright green eyeshadow and lashes to match.

"You look mint," Angel says. "He's not going to know what hit him."

I'm still not sure. I'm not even sure he likes me.

"What if he don't want to kiss me?" I ask. "Do I lose the dare?"

"Just kiss *him*," says Angel, as if it's that easy. "Or kiss someone. How long since you broke up with Prince Parker or whatever 'is name is? Months?"

I shrug, to cover the shiver. "Something like that."

"So, it's like riding a bike, innit. You fall off, you need to get back in the saddle."

"S'pose."

"No s'pose about it. Now come on. Give us a smile."

I pull my best crazy-lady face.

"Ash, come on."

I smile, proper this time. Like I'm smiling at Seamus. One side of my mouth higher than the other so my dimple shows and I'm dead cute. I know 'cause I practised in front of the mirror before.

"Knockout, babe. You look knockout. Ready?"

We're at Kel's door now, and I can hear the music coming from inside, and the laughing and the yelps of the little ones. I feel it again. The pull of velocity as the carriage I'm stuck in lurches forward on the ride. My skin's sweating and my stomach's queasy and I'm hot, too hot. But it's too late to back out now. I said I'd do the dare and I will. I'll kiss him. Or someone. Just a peck on the cheek, I reckon. That's still a kiss, isn't it?

"Ready as I'll ever be," I say.

But I don't feel ready. I don't feel ready at all.

Ten

I wanted it to be like in a film. So we'd all be inside waiting, dead quiet, the curtains drawn. Then Kel's dad would come in the door and we'd all burst out, "Surprise, surprise," and he'd be astonished and there'd be crying and hugging and this big ballad on the stereo. Only when we get in, he's already on the sofa with Liam on his lap and a can of Stella in his hand and the stereo's playing Sharon's One Direction CD. I know it's him 'cause Kel showed me the photos of him and his brothers. I scan the room but

117

I can only see one of them and I reckon he must be Ronan's dad 'cause he got the same slicked-back hair and smarm. I don't think about where the other is – the other Dooley – 'cause that only makes the ride go faster and steeper.

I don't reckon anyone's thinking too much about him neither, 'cause they're all smiling. Kel's mum most of all. I never seen her like this. She's dancing with Jake, holding his hands so he can jump up and down, and her hair's done and she's got make-up on, and a bra and all. I try not to notice the cigarette in her mouth 'cause that spoils it a bit. Instead I smile, and try not to let on that I feel like the odd one out. Like I shouldn't be here, 'cause they're all family, all part of the gang. Even Angel, 'cause she's been coming round here since forever. And anyway, she kind of shines in a way that means she's never out of place. But me, not even my skin fits. Only then I hear it.

"Ash!" I turn, and there's Kel. She throws her arms round me and I almost choke on body spray.

"Babe!" It's Angel's turn now and they're all over each other like Angel's been gone as long as Kel's dad, instead of the couple of hours since we went down Crackerjack for Cokes. "They here?"

"Upstairs." She gestures over her shoulder and we follow, picking our way through the sea of dogs and Dooleys, so many Dooleys. But even so, I feel that spark; the dare, yeah, but the being part of it, even if I don't know if we're Socs or Greasers or something else entirely.

They're in Kel's bedroom – Ronan and Seamus – and there's two girls and all, older, sixteen or seventeen maybe. One of them must be Siobhan, I reckon. The one who's supposed to have set this up. The one who's sizing me up like I'm a pound of ham.

"Everyone, this is Asha," Kel says.

Seamus looks up and nods and I do the smile, only it don't feel cute now, it feels awkward.

"All right," Ronan says. "Ash."

"All right," I echo back.

"Asha, this is everyone. And you know Angel."

"Everyone knows Angel," says Ronan. And she flashes him a look that's half fake anger, half *come and get me*.

"Budge up, Shev," says Kel, and the girl who was eyeing me moves along the bunk so me and Kel can squish in. Angel sits next to Ronan, bold as brass and bent forward just enough so he can see right down her top.

"She'll get nowhere," says Kel to me as we watch her pull all the tricks out of the bag – fingering her necklace, touching his leg, giggling at his every word. "He's been there already. She's used goods, innit."

Right then I don't believe her. 'Cause why wouldn't he want to snog her, and more. She looks like a model. Not a super one maybe, but still, a model. But by half ten she's dirty dancing with only a crop top on, and he's still not tried it on once.

But then nor has Seamus.

"You want another Coke, Ash?" Kel asks.

I shake my head. I've had four already and a load of Fanta and I feel a bit weird, like I've had half a tonne of Haribo and I'm buzzing and sick at the same time.

"Angel?"

Angel looks at me, then at Ronan and Seamus who're in the corner doing something on Ronan's phone. "I'll come with you, innit. Give Ash some air."

And then they're gone and it's just me and the boys 'cause Shev and Donna – that's the other girl – are in the downstairs loo 'cause Donna thought her Bacardi Breezers were J2Os and now they're making a reappearance.

And I know no one's going to be here to see it happen, but I got to do it soon, 'cause I'm due home in half an hour. I checked on Kel's phone. Mine's downstairs in my jacket 'cause this dress hasn't got any room for pockets. Besides, maybe this is one thing I don't want an audience for. I shuffle my bum

121

off the bed and onto the floor so I'm near them.

"What are you playing?" I ask.

Seamus answers without looking up. "*Temple Run*," he says.

"Give us a go, then," I say.

Ronan looks over at me. "You played before?"

"No. But how hard can it be? You two can do it," I sass.

Seamus looks up, then back at the phone. "Shit. I lost."

"My turn then," I say and I push my legs in between them so we're like sardines in a row, and hold my hand out.

Seamus looks at Ronan who just shrugs. But his eyes are on me as Seamus hands the phone over.

"What've I got to do?" I ask.

"Seriously?" Seamus says.

"Here," says Ronan, shooting him a look. "I'll show you."

He scoots round so he's next to me, his hips touching mine. My legs look bare against his skinny jeans. They *are* bare. I wish I hadn't worn this dress now. You can probably see my knickers from where Seamus's sat. I look over at him but he's fiddling with the iPod dock looking for tunes.

"You got to move this up and down, yeah?"

I nod. Do as I'm told.

"No," he puts his finger on mine. "Keep it held down and don't let go 'til the last second. That's it!"

He lifts his finger and pulls mine with it and the thing that's me in the game jumps and clears the crevasse.

"Nice one," I say.

"You're getting it," he says. I risk a glance at him and see he's smiling. A proper smile. Not like Angel's, which always means something more than *I'm happy*, always has something else thrown in.

"Concentrate," he says.

I flick my eyes back to the phone. But I'm not concentrating, not on the game anyway.

I feel Seamus lift himself up off the floor.

"Where you going?" asks Ronan.

"See a man about a dog," Seamus replies.

I look up then. 'Cause I heard that saying before, from Otis and Ellis and on telly too. And it could be anything from having a pee to doing some deal. I hear an explosion from the phone and I know I've lost. That game anyway.

"You coming back?" I ask.

Seamus looks at Ronan as if he's going to give him the answer. "In a bit," he says.

A bit. That could be ten minutes. Or it could be an hour. I don't have that long.

I go to stand but Ronan pulls me down. "Don't," he says. "Have another go."

"I—"

"Just one," he interrupts.

And he seems serious. Like he'd be sad if I didn't. "All right," I say. "Just one. 'Cause I got to go soon, innit."

"Why? You gonna turn into a pumpkin like Cinderella or something?"

"Ha ha," I mock-laugh. "Anyway it was the coach

that turned into a pumpkin. Cinderella just went back to rags."

His eyes drop down to the dress, then back to mine. "I wouldn't care," he says.

Then I feel it proper. A first big spin. And I know it's too late, I can't get off. And I know what's going to happen.

I start up the game like that might stop it, or slow it, but his hand reaches up and touches my face and I crash and burn before I'm even past the first leap.

"Ash," he says. His voice is different now. Lower. And I look at him and I see what they all see. That he's someone. And I should want him. And part of me does. And Angel, she said it didn't matter who, I just got to kiss someone. And even though I know she didn't mean Ronan, I know I'm going to do it.

And then it's happening. No warning, one minute he's looking at me a bit funny and next thing his mouth's on mine and his tongue's pushing at my lips. I don't know what to do 'cause Joe never kissed me like this before. In the end I let him and it feels all wet, like a jellied eel from Manze's on the corner of Peckham Park Road. Only a warm one. And it's not horrible. Just different.

He puts his hand on my hip and I feel it slide up and I know which base he's heading to. I grab it and push it down again, back to my hip.

He don't seem to notice though, he's just kissing me harder and then his hand's back and it's higher this time and I'm just about to push it away or say no or something when I hear a voice saying, "Cheese," and then a flash and I look up and there's Kel in the doorway with her iPhone out and mouth gaping open and Angel behind her with a face like she don't know if she's gonna slap me or him first. The ride crashes to a sickening, screeching halt.

I scramble up, pull my dress down.

"What the—" Ronan starts.

"I . . . Shit. I'm sorry, Ang. I didn't . . ." But she's stormed off down the stairs.

"Blimey, Ash. Didn't know you had it in you," says Kel.

126

"She's going to kill me," I say.

"No she's not," says Kel.

"You better delete that," says Ronan to Kel.

"Why?" she says. "Who's going make me?"

"Just do it," he says. "You know why."

"Yeah I do, and they're DDs and stuck on the front of Keris Coleman."

Ronan shakes his head. "Bunch of kids," he says, and pushes past Kel out the door. And I know I've blown it with him, not that I want to see him again anyway, not with Angel on my case.

It's just me and Kel now. "I'm sorry," I say.

"Not me you got to say it to," says Kel. "Don't matter to me. But I'd give it 'til tomorrow, yeah?"

Eleven

I change my dress in the downstairs loo, put
Angel's in a bag to give to her on Monday. It smells
of sick in there and I have to hold my breath when
I do it. I might as well not have bothered though,
'cause my face is still plastered with make-up and
when I check my phone as I walk round the corner
to Lyndhurst there's a text from Patience saying *go
home* and four missed calls and all of them from Otis.
For just a second I think maybe something's
happened to Mum. But when I walk in the flat Otis
got a face on him that don't look sad, just angry,

and disappointed. And I don't know which is worse.

He don't say anything at first, just stares at me. And I think maybe he's just going to send me to my room and that'll be it. But I don't get away so easy.

"Where you been, chile?"

I feel my heart bang-banging in my chest. "I-I told you," I stammer. "Church thing, innit."

"I called Mr Williams."

I feel my heart slip and thud down into my belly, churning all the Coke up. "Oh," is all I can get out.

"Oh?" Otis shakes his head. "You know Patience answer the phone. I asked where her dad and she say he asleep. So I ask how come you not home then if church group over. She say you be back soon enough."

"I . . ." I try to think something up quick. But my head is too busy dealing with what Patience did.

"You get your friends to lie for you now too?"

"No," I say. "I never asked her. She just . . ."

"Well, she one good friend then."

I shrug.

"That all you got to say for yourself?"

Normally words is what I got; words come so quickly I can't stop them pouring out, clatter-clatter, one on top of the other. Now I can hardly drag one up from inside me. "Sorry," I manage.

Otis nods. "So if you not at church, where were you?"

Then the words come. "This girl's house," I say. "Kelly Dooley, she's in my year. There was this party – her dad's, 'cause he's been away and now he's back, innit. I didn't drink anything, only Coke. Or smoke neither," I add.

"Been away where?" asks Otis.

I know what he's thinking 'cause he knows the name just like I do. He knows what they done to Joe, and what he done to them.

"Work," I say. "Building up Newcastle. It's not . . . He's not . . ." but I can't say the words out loud.

"Who else was with you?" Otis says. "Just this Kelly?"

"No," I say. "Some others. Angel Jones, she's in my

year and all. And Kelly's cousins . . ." My voice trails off again as a picture of that kiss snaps into my head like the flash on a camera phone.

"So why you don't tell me? Tell your mum?"

"You know what she's like," I say. That she got no friends, not now. The ones from back here think she's too big for her boots, the ones at work think her boots are too shoddy. And the ones where we moved, she don't like those stay-at-home women. Lazy, she calls them. And crazy. Relying on a man for money. She don't speak to them and they don't speak to her. And what she sees in them, she's going to see in Angel and Kelly, and more besides. She's going to see their make-up and their smart mouths and dirty talk. She's going to see Angel's easy money and Kelly's none. Going to see their mums, all the kids, the dogs, Fat Brian, all of it. Not really looking, just seeing what she wants to see. And none of it good.

And I know Otis knows all this too, 'cause all he says is, "You lucky she asleep."

"No change there, then," I say.

"Asha." He shakes his head. "You know what it like for her. And she trying. But you got to try too. This a chance for you to spend time together. Get to know each other."

I don't get it. "She's my mum, innit. Of course I know her. And she's not trying. She's the same as she always was, only lying down instead of always out the door."

"You really know her? Or you just know the story you like to tell? That she care more about those kids in court than she do for you? 'Cause that's not true. She work hard to do that and it's a good job, an important job. You should be proud."

I don't say anything to that. Don't even move a muscle. 'Cause I know he's right that it's a good job. But it don't mean I have to like it.

"It's late," he says eventually. "You get to bed now."

I nod. I'm tired. Tired proper 'cause I'm worn out from the night, and tired of this talking too.

"And do me one favour?" Otis asks. Though I can hear it's not really a question at all.

And I wait for it. For him to say that I'm going to have to 'fess it all up to Mum or I'm grounded until I'm eighteen or that I got to stop seeing Kelly and Angel, though I might have managed that all by myself anyway. But instead he got just two words.

"Be safe," he says.

I will, I think. *I am*.

But as I lie on my bed, looking out the window at the lights on Crackerjack, and the city beyond, my head full of that kiss and Angel's face in the doorway and what Joe's going to say when he finds out, I don't feel safe at all. Not one bit.

I stay in bed past lunch on Sunday. Tell Otis I'm not feeling well so he brings me toast and a bowl of chicken soup in bed, but I can tell from the look on his face that he don't think it's the flu that's ailing me, and I can tell I got to get up soon and all.

It's three o'clock by the time I go into the front room. Mum and Otis are on the sofa watching a film, this old one in black and white where they all talk proper and the kids are dressed in suits and dresses like shrunken grown-ups, and not one of them talks back.

There's a space next to Mum but I sit down on the green chair instead. The one Otis says Grandma used to sit in, to knit and listen to the radio and look out the window at the small small world.

I try watching the telly for a bit but too much has gone by already and I don't want to ask what's happening 'cause Mum will only sigh, and I can't be bothered to make up the plot like I normally do. Besides, someone else isn't watching either 'cause I can feel his eyes on me.

"Joe called," he says. "You supposed to be seeing him today?"

My stomach flip-flops. We were supposed to meet up at his. He wanted to see the stuffed walrus in the museum, and the aquarium. We seen them a hundred times before but he never gets bored of it. "I forgot," I say.

I go to check my phone and there's a text from

him too. Nothing from Angel though, even though I texted her three times to say sorry and I wrote *sorry* forty times and all. Maybe her phone's out of battery, I tell myself. Or it got nicked, or she dropped it down the toilet. But I know I'm just lying to myself.

"You should call him," Mum says then.

I look at Otis, as if he's going to tell me what's going on 'cause she never wants me to ring Joe. She don't even like me seeing him and only says I can 'cause his social worker and Otis say I'm good for him. "I—" I start. But I don't get a chance to get the words out 'cause the phone starts to ring like it's been listening in. And I know who it is, because only one person calls the landline. And Mum knows it too.

"That'll be him," she says. "You can get that."

"But I don't want to talk to him," I say. "Not right now."

Only Otis and Mum aren't moving and there's no answerphone so in the end it's me who gets up and picks up the receiver.

"Hello?" I say, and I do this thing, like I'm bracing myself to be slapped. I wait for Joe's voice and his *why*s and *why-didn't-you*s to buzz into my ears like angry bees.

But when the "hello" comes back from the other end of the line, it's not Joe's voice at all, but a man's.

"Asha?" he says.

"Ellis?" I reply.

"Yes," he says. Then goes quiet. He never was much good at talking to me, or any kids for that matter. He don't do family law like Mum, not any more. He does businesses going bust or managers stealing from bosses. Corporate law, it's called. Not much feeling in that. Not much small talk.

"You want to speak to Mum?" I ask him.

"Yes," he says, and I hear the hope in just three letters.

But when I hold the receiver out to Mum I see she's shaking her head.

I put it back to my ear. "She don't want to talk to

you," I say. And I hang up before he can even ask why.

"He call a lot for someone who don't want you," says Otis.

Mum shrugs and turns her head away.

Then Otis looks at me. "You both as bad as each other. Not talking to them. You don't know what they got to say unless you listen."

But Mum isn't listening even now. She turns up the volume on the telly and makes like she's dead interested in what the woman in the massive hat has got to say.

I know she heard him though. And I know she's thinking about Ellis. That it not just the cancer that's left a hole in her, but the loss of him and all.

I text Joe later that night. Say I'm sorry and that I don't feel well but maybe we can do it next Sunday instead.

Can't do Sunday, he says back. *My nan's coming. I told you.*

JOANNA NADIN

And I feel sick all over again 'cause he did tell me, and I know that's a big thing for him and his mum, that they haven't seen her in years.

Saturday then? I say.

OK, he says.

And then, a few seconds later, an *x*.

I feel warm then, like I'm swimming in soup. I read once that that's what love's supposed to feel like. Not like a fairground ride or champagne and lobsters, but like a cup of tea or a jacket potato. Warm and familiar. Like it won't let you down. Or make you sick.

And I send him an *x* back.

But when I check my phone an hour later and Angel's not replied still I can't feel the potato anymore, just a hole like Mum's got, and coldness creeping in. So I do what I always do. I pick up my book and bury myself in story, glorious story. I read until it's so real I can feel myself right there in Ponyboy's house, smelling the eggs and chocolate cake he's cooking for breakfast, and smoke from

138

Two-Bit's cigarettes. McCardle's right, I think, that books get you through stuff. And I wonder then what this one got him through. Was he just lying on his bed like me, shut up in his bedroom, all pissed at a friend, or was he shut up somewhere else? And then I start making up my own story for him, that he's lying low in a church somewhere, or an abandoned house – that's it, an abandoned house. And he's hiding not from police but from his own friends, a gang who've turned on him just for reading, like, just for thinking words are weapons, good as guns. And I wonder, then, if life really could turn out like a story I wrote. Or even if I could change my own life by writing it different, change what's happening right now – Mum and the cancer, Ellis, Angel, Joe, all of it. Only then I think that words may be weapons, but a pen isn't the same thing as a magic wand.

Not even close.

Twelve

I don't reckon I believe in God. Not really. 'Cause the Bible's full of mad stuff like people being turned into salt and water being turned into wine, and if you got your period you got to go and sit in a hut by yourself. Plus there's no way God created the world in seven days, it's the Big Bang and evolution, innit, I've seen the dinosaur skeletons and the fossils in museums and no one mentions them in Genesis or Exodus.

Only when I wake up on Monday, I got God and

Patience on my mind. 'Cause I know how much it cost her to do what she did for me: lying like that. That's against the Ten Commandments and she's probably thinking she's going to be punished or go to hell or something. So I need to say thanks to her and sorry and that she can tell God it's all down to me, and if he thinks about it he should be praising her for doing a good deed to thy neighbour. Only when I get out the front door she's not waiting on the wall like she usually is so I have to walk to school by myself. I look for Angel and Kel as well only it's raining so they're not out front holding court, they're inside somewhere in another form room and I figure that conversation can wait 'cause that's the harder one anyway and I got to work up to it. But Patience isn't as easy to talk to as I thought 'cause when I slide in next to her she don't say anything, just carries on pretending to be absorbed in *Animal Farm* and I know she's not really reading 'cause she finished that book last week, same as me.

"All right?" I say.

She still don't say anything.

"Thanks. For what you did, I mean. Telling Otis all that stuff." I can't say "lies" 'cause that makes it worse. It's a story anyway. Just a story.

She shrugs then.

"Did he believe me?" she says, still looking at her book.

"No," I say and I laugh even though it wasn't funny, not really.

Patience don't think it's funny either. "Were you in trouble?"

"A bit," I say. "He didn't tell my mum though, so it could be worse."

"That's good," she says and turns the page.

And that's the end of that conversation. She don't ask who I was with or what I was doing. Maybe she don't care. Or maybe she already knows. But something's changed 'cause when I go to sit with her at lunch she looks away and starts talking to Dennis and the grinning twins and I know she's saying she don't want me there any more. I don't even go near

Angel and Kel. I saw them on the corridor in break and I was going to go over but Kel shook her head like she was saying, "Don't even think about it if you want to live." Then I texted her and she said Angel's told her she can't talk to me until she says so, so I got to delete her text and all, but that she'll put in a good word 'cause she knows it weren't all me, it were mostly Ronan 'cause he can't keep his hands or his tongue to himself. So I do what she says and delete the text, and I stay away and sit by myself and pretend I like it like that.

But I don't. There's no fun making up stories about the teachers if no one's there to laugh when you do it. And there's no fun partnering LaTia Brown in netball 'cause she don't want to talk about ghosts or monsters or last night's telly, she wants to actually play the game and then she slams the ball so hard into your chest it knocks the air out of you. And there's no fun seeing Ronan by the lockers laughing with Seamus and then he sees you and stops his sniggering and looks at you like you're the dirt on his shoe instead, and there's no one to tell or to agree he's not worth it.

And the next day I can't stay away anyway, 'cause it's English.

She's watching me when I walk in, waiting to see what I do. But there's only one seat going and it's on her row. Only she's made Kel budge up so I can't sit between them any more like the jam in a sandwich, I'm on the end, with Kel a barbed-wire fence between us. I figure I'll be all right though, 'cause all she's done so far is ignore me and whatever the magazines say, being ignored is not worse than being talked about, if being talked about means Angel Jones is slagging you off and calling you a slapper.

Only, ten minutes in and it looks like Angel's had a change of heart. McCardle's got us talking about *Lord of the Flies* and how it's like the riots, 'cause loads of kids got involved who'd never done anything bad before, they just got easily led. And that's when Angel starts in.

"You want to ask Asha about that, sir. She'll do anything Ronan Dooley tells her."

"Ang!" says Kel. But I don't know if she's shocked or laughing, 'cause I don't turn to look at them and I don't say anything either.

"Seriously, sir. She's like Piggy, innit."

"That's enough, Angel," says McCardle.

But she carries on making pig noises every few minutes until everyone's in stitches and in the end McCardle sends her out to see the Head.

"Thanks," she says to me, as she pushes past my chair so the edge of the desk rams hard into my stomach.

Kel don't say anything still, but before the end of the lesson I feel her nudge me and I look and she's written inside the cover of her book. *She'll come round*, it says. And I want to believe her, but Wednesday's just as bad. It's like I've brought on a plague of sadness or something 'cause everyone's fighting. The only person who's happy is Kelley Eckersley 'cause she's back with Seamus. Stacey saw

145

them on a bench outside the library eating a McFlurry and snogging yesterday afternoon. It must be true 'cause Kelley's stopped with the emo stuff and in writing group she offers me a Malteser but I don't take one 'cause I feel bad about what I was going to do with Seamus.

McCardle's in a right mood and all. He makes us come up with a story about a hero or a villain. You got to put down everything about them, what they look like, smell like, where they live, what they did in their childhood. Backstory, he calls it.

I do one about a villain called Boris Kalashnikov. He's this great sweaty pirate with a beard like a bird's nest, and all the sailors are afraid of him. They tell tales about how he grates the soles of his victims' feet, and lets rats gnaw your fingers and puts burning rope under his hat to make him look fiercer. And he didn't have a childhood 'cause he was raised by wolves in some woods in Russia.

I think it's dead good, like a proper horror story, but after I finish reading it out to everyone

McCardle's shaking his head and he's got that look on his face like Otis sometimes has, like he don't know whether to be angry or disappointed.

"You've seen too many films," he says. "All of you. Villains don't go round twirling their moustaches or laughing like ... like hyenas. They don't have a badge on them saying 'I'm bad'. Villains arrive as your friend. They say what you want to hear so you trust them, so you like them. Then they stick the knife in. Believe me, I've been there, and it hurts twice as bad when it's your best mate with the handle in their fingers."

"Was you actually stabbed, sir?" this kid called Marvin asks.

I sort of flinch at this, remembering Johnnycake and the Soc, remembering what I made up in my head, about McCardle hiding out. Maybe McCardle did stab someone. Or maybe he was just one of the gang who helped it happen. Whichever, I'm not going to find out now.

"*Were* you," says McCardle. "*Were* you stabbed.

147

And that's not the point. The knife doesn't have to be real. It can be a word, or a look, or just being ignored, but it still digs deep."

And he looks straight at me when he says that. And I know what he's trying to say: that Angel's the villain. That she got previous – a bad backstory – and she look like the bitch in a teen film, all glossy and hard at the edges. But I don't think he's watched enough films, 'cause if he had he'd know that sometimes the villain turns out to be the good guy after all. And Angel, she's not had a bad childhood. So her mum's a bit OCD and her dad went off, but he sends her stuff all the time. Even Fat Brian gives her presents. If anyone's going to be the villain it should be me or Patience, and even though she still not talking to me I know it ain't her. So that leaves me. And I know I did some things wrong but I don't feel bad, not villain bad.

And the next day I know I'm right, 'cause I'm sitting eating my sandwich on a table with Marvin and the other chess club kids when Angel slips into the chair next to me and offers me a curly fry like Saturday never happened. And then Kel's there and all, and she's talking to Marvin about some game they had, and Angel's asking me who'd I rather, Prince Harry or Prince William, and we're all laughing and it's like the end of a film where the geeks and the popular kids all hug and make up. For thirty-five minutes anyway, 'cause then the bell goes and they've all disappeared 'cause they can't be late for maths so it's just me and Kel and Angel left.

"So, you want to come over after school?" Angel says.

"Sure," I say, all casual-like. 'Cause I'm not going to act like she handed me the winning lottery numbers or something.

"Laters then." She pushes the chip plate away and stands up, motions to Kelly to follow.

"Laters," I say.

And as I take the plate to the dirty-tray stacks, Kel looks back at me, and I wonder if it's a trick, like in

McCardle's version, but she's smiling so I can see the black tooth, and I know it's going to be all right.

And it is, because by Friday night, we're like Charlie's Angels again, doing our hair and painting our lips and taking the pee out of Seamus and Kelley for holding hands in the canteen queue. We're not villains, we're superheroes, saving the world – or Peckham – from boredom. And I'm so full of joy and relief I don't think to ask why she's let me back in.

"You know what we should do?" says Angel, as she draws a perfect flick on my eyelid in liquid liner.

"What?" asks Kel, flipping through *Heat*, checking out celebrity cellulite.

"We should go up West, innit. Celebrate 'cause we're all back together. We could do it tomorrow. Ash, you up for it?"

Tomorrow's Saturday and I'm supposed to be meeting Joe. But this, this is more important, isn't it? If I say no, she'll drop me for good and then I won't have anyone again. Besides, what are me and Joe going to do? Hang about the museum again looking at dead animals behind glass? Where's the fun in that? I'll think of an excuse. I'll make it up to him. But this, this is golden. This is the ticket, and I got to do it.

"I got to check at home," I say. "But, yeah, I'm in."

She nods. "Kel?"

Kelly looks up from a picture of someone off *TOWIE* with a red ring around her thighs. "Long as I'm not flaming babysitting," she says and goes back to the mag. "Christ. If I ever get legs like that, you might as well shoot me."

It's not just Joe I got to deal with though, it's Otis. And Mum. But I got a plan. I'm going to be bold, like a Charlie's Angel, like Angel, even. I'm going to act like going up Oxford Street's nothing and that Kel and Angel aren't the bad girls McCardle or Mum reckon, they're just girls. And that's not even acting, it's not lies. It's truth.

When I get in there's stew on the stove and Otis is setting the table in the living room.

"That smells good," I say.

Otis looks up and raises an eyebrow. "What you after, girl?" he asks.

"Nothing," I say, pinching a piece of bread out of the bowl. "It's all right if I go up West tomorrow, isn't it? Only I told the girls I would, so it'd be letting them down if I back out now."

Mum looks up from the crappy quiz show she's watched every day for the last month. "What girls?" she asks. "And what for? You haven't got any money."

"Just to look at stuff," I say, and sit down in my place, 'cause I know Otis is bringing the pot in any minute.

"You didn't answer the other question," she says.

"Didn't I?" I ask. "Oh, Kelly and Angel. They're in my English class." And I think that'll do it 'cause she knows I'm in top English and Patience is too.

Only I forget she's good at maths even when her

brain's been fried with chemicals, 'cause she puts two and two together and makes four straight off.

"Angel Jones?" she says and I know she's raising an eyebrow and all, even if it is an invisible one 'cause painting it on is pointless these days.

"Yeah," I say, still playing it down. "She's dead nice now. Totally changed. Her mum don't work in the bookies any more, neither, she works up West in one of the department stores. Debenhams. Dead glam."

"*Doesn't* work," she corrects. And I know she's thinking up what to say about Debenhams, that it's not like being a lawyer, it's not even like working in Harvey Nicks, but Otis got something to say and he gets in there first.

"I thought you seeing Joe tomorrow."

"I am," I say. "Was, I mean. He had to cancel. Seeing his nan."

"What about Patience?" he asks. "She going?"

I shake my head. "Not her thing," I say. Though I don't even know what her thing is apart from God and reading.

I eat a mouthful of stew and gag. "Nice," I lie. "Lamb."

Otis nods. "Your mum say you like it."

I nod. "So, can I?"

Mum sighs, like even answering a question is too much for her right now. "I'll think about it," she says.

And I smile and swallow another mouthful, even though I hate lamb, and have done since I was five.

Angel texts at ten that night. *You coming or what?*

I'm working on it, I say.

Don't let me down, comes back.

I won't, I reply.

And I won't. 'Cause I know what'll happen if I do.

Thirteen

And I don't, because, without me even trying to write it, without me waving a magic wand, Mum says yes.

Otis has worked on her. Told her to think back to when she was thirteen and up West every Saturday with Shaniqua and Julie, coming back with their Topshop bags and their smiles wider than a mile. She sucked her teeth at that. "That's what I'm worried about," she said.

But she must reckon he's got a point 'cause she

says OK, or rather, she gives me a list of rules that make the Ten Commandments look half-hearted: no smoking, no piercing, no going down the skate park in the tunnels by the river, no cheeking, no staying out past dark. *What about breathing?* I want to say. But I don't, 'cause I'm just glad she gave in in the end and I don't want her to swallow it back and spit out a big fat no instead.

Then there's just Joe to work on. I text him to say Mum's bad and I got to stay in and help 'cause Otis is on shift. He is too, so it's not all a story, and Joe don't know that Mum got off the sofa and made tea this morning. Otis says it's a good sign but I think he's hoping too much. She has tea when she's glad and when she's lost the biggest case. Tea's just tea, it don't change the world and it don't predict the future, whatever Mrs Joyful King reckons.

Joe texts back straight away. *So sorry, Ash. Can I do anything?*

No, don't worry, I type quick. *Got it covered.*

And I have. 'Cause by ten I'm outside Crackerjack

in my jeans with my smile already half a mile and a tenner from Otis burning a hole in my pocket.

Kel's the first to arrive, even though I can see Angel's front room window from where I'm standing, and she's ten minutes late as it is.

"Sorry, our Sharon was in the bathroom and wouldn't come out 'cause Lacey something or other said she's fat, and Liam's stuck Jake's Furby down the downstairs bog so that's out of bounds. Had to go down McDonald's in the end just for a pee."

She could have come round mine, I think. If she knew where I lived. If Mum wasn't there. If the flat didn't smell of Dettol and sickness. But that's too many ifs.

"They let you in without getting anything?"

"Didn't say I didn't get anything, did I," she says and pulls two hash browns out of her pockets. "Want one?"

"You're not hungry?"

"Didn't say that neither, but I already had two sausage McMuffins coming up Rye Lane."

"Ta," I say and take one.

That tapeworm's going to explode one day, I think as I take a bite of the hot, crispy potato. It'll be like a scene in an alien film where it bursts through an eyeball or out her belly button. She'll be nothing but worm and a shrivelled Kelly skin lying on the floor like when a snake sheds its scales.

"Nice, breakfast," says a voice behind me, as a ring-covered gel-nailed hand reaches over my shoulder and snatches the hash brown.

Angel.

"Thought you were on a diet," I say.

"You telling me I'm fat?" says Angel, mid-chew.

"As if," says Kel, before I can get in.

"Now Patience Williams, she could do with staying out of Maccy D's," says Angel. "Must be hard when it's only next door though."

"I don't think she goes in," I say.

"Why?" says Angel. "God tell her not to?"

I shrug.

"Anyway, how do you know? You joined the God squad and all?"

"No," I say. "Just, you know, guessing. She always has packed lunch."

"What, you mean you don't talk about how Jesus wants you for a sunbeam and stuff in your little writing group?" Angel's got her eyebrow arched and her hand on her hip.

"Piss off, Ang," says Kel.

"Yeah, piss off," I say, testing it out.

Angel's mouth drops open and I'm wishing I hadn't said it or that the ground would open up and swallow me or a bolt of lightning would crackle out of the sky and spark off the bus stop so she forgets it. But in the end what comes out isn't a scream or a swear word but a laugh.

"Bloody hell, Ash, didn't think you had that in you," she smiles. "Welcome to my world."

"We getting on the twelve or what?" says Kel.

And then we're all laughing and squealing and swearing and bustling onboard, clattering up the stairs to get the front seats and the best view and be queens of all we survey.

For a day anyway.

Most people hate the journey; moan and gripe and can't wait to get where they're going. Not Joe though – he loves buses; the numbers, the routes, all of it. Otis too. He says buses are full of tales; that they carry spies and thieves and all life to work and play and home again. He used to take me to work with him sometimes, let me sit on the back seat and I used to make up stories about the other passengers, pretend the man in the hat was an evil overlord heading to his underground lair, or that the lady with the sad eyes and the soggy dog at her feet was a princess in disguise. Today I don't need make-believe nor Otis, and I'm glad it's not his bus 'cause we're full of it, already at the fair, the bus is our roller coaster and we're screaming at the joy of it. I look out the window at the sights flying past and know that this is where I'm going to be in thirteen years: In my office at the Houses of Parliament, changing laws and making history; at the theatres and cinemas on Shaftesbury Avenue – words I've written making thousands of people cry and laugh and be somewhere else, be other people for a night; then after I'd go up Regent Street buying my Jimmy Choos and my Christian Dior. Up West is where life is. And for just a few minutes I get why Mum wanted to escape, even if it was to Epping not Oxford Circus.

"This is us," says Ang. "Come on."

I look out the window as we lurch to a halt in the Saturday crowds and I feel it in me, dancing in my belly, stamping in my heart and lungs in its silver-soled shoes: adventure. This is what I love, and why I love Ang and Kel. Today's an adventure and we didn't have to go to sea and fight pirates to have it. We just had to get the number twelve.

And it is an adventure. We eat burgers for lunch and even though they're the same Big Macs you get in

161

Peckham or Old Kent Road or even up Essex, they taste different here, like they're made from special cows or got gold in them.

"You can eat gold," I say. And it's true. I've seen it in champagne glasses and on cakes.

"Does it come out the same?" asks Kel. "Like do you have glitter in your poo?"

And we laugh and pretend to be sick and Ang tells us about the time she swallowed a diamond and her mum had to dig through her nappy to get it back and we all groan again. After, we go see Ang's mum in Debenhams, all tanned and shining in her uniform suit and uniform make-up, and she does our eyes for us and gives us free samples of bronzer which doesn't do much for me so I give mine to Kel and she swaps it for a bubblegum. Then we're blowing pink balloons up and down Carnaby Street and into Topshop where we try on bikinis and boob tubes and mini-skirts and maxi-dresses and Angel puts on a white one, full length, and says she'll wear it when she marries Prince Charming.

"Prince Chav more like," says Kel.

"That word's banned," says Ang. "McCardle says so."

"Well, marry him instead," says Kel. "I know you want to."

"Piss off!" shrieks Angel and then they're throwing clothes at each other and laughing so much Kel says she might be sick. But she's not. Nothing bad happens. Ang buys some knickers and I get a pair of socks 'cause that's all the money I got left from Otis's tenner and Kel doesn't get anything but she says she don't mind, she's having a ball anyway.

And that's when we take a wrong turn in the adventure 'cause suddenly we're not in paradise anymore or the enchanted kingdom, we're in trouble. And it starts with that look in Angel's eyes.

"I got an idea," she says.

"Now we're screwed," says Kel, only she's smiling when she says it.

"Oh, ha ha," says Ang. "I know Ash is up for it anyway."

163

"Up for what?" I ask, only I don't need to. I know what she's going to say before she's even thought it.

"Dare," she says. "I dare you to nick something."

"Who, me?" says Kel.

"All of us," Angel says.

"I'm all right," says Kel. "I'm not bothered if I don't get stuff, I told you, innit."

"Bullshit," says Ang.

"Bull true," says Kel, squaring up to her.

But it only takes one word from Ang to change her mind.

"Chicken," she says.

And Kel rolls her eyes and huffs and says, "Whatever. Fine."

"Nice one. Ash?"

I feel sick and I don't know if it's the burger and milkshake or the buzz or 'cause I don't want to or 'cause I do. And I know what it'd do to Mum – me breaking the law and her being a barrister and all. But right now she's barely a mum, let alone a law-maker. And there's only one answer anyway, if I want to keep Ang, if I want to sit with her and Kel in class and go round her house after. And even if I did fancy going back to Patience and the happy-clappers I don't think they'd have me anyway.

So I say the only word I can. I say, "Yes."

And the buzz when I do almost buckles my knees.

We pick the make-up counter 'cause the stuff there's small and it's busy and what's a six quid nail varnish when you've got hundred-pound dresses downstairs. Ang's so swift she's done before I've even started looking; a lipstick dropped down her top so it's caught above the waist of her jeans. She could be a professional, I think – a hustler like on telly. She's got the looks, she could fool anyone.

Kel's slower, waiting for the security guy to check out some girls messing with the tights before she picks a green nail varnish and jams it in her pocket.

"You're never going to wear that," says Ang, shaking her head.

"Not the point," says Kel, "is it."

She's right. But even so I take my time, fingers lingering over the eyeliners in blue and green and a purple so deep it looks like wine. In the end I pick a gold one that'll really show up, that I could wear down Chicago's, if they ever let me in.

Kel's not even looking; she's too busy trying blusher out, big pink streaks across her pale cheeks. Angel's watching though, eyes on my hands as she fiddles with a foundation packet. "Nice one," she says.

I turn it over, checking for alarm codes but there're none, which makes it their fault if you think about it, that's what Ang said earlier, so there's nothing stopping me, not really. Except that when I try to put it in a pocket or in my bag I can't seem to move.

"Hurry up," says Ang. "I need a pee."

"Me and all," says Kel, looking in the tiny smeared mirror and rubbing at her face. "Too much Coke, innit."

I check round again, making sure no one else's got

their eyes on me, but it's clear, there's too many people anyway on Saturday, you could steal a handbag probably, a hat even. And I can feel Kel jiggling now, needing the loo, so I swallow down the scared and the feeble I'm feeling and I stick that eyeliner in my pocket, bold as you like, then I turn and walk nice and slow straight out the doors onto Oxford Street.

But I only get two steps away when I hear something behind me. A scuffle and a voice – a man's – saying "Oi!"

Shit, I think, and my stomach pitches like I have eaten a gone-off sausage after all. "Keep walking," I say to myself. "Don't turn round, don't turn round."

But I can't help it. It's like that door in the horror film the heroine knows she shouldn't open because bad things are behind it, but she does it anyway. So I look over my shoulder, fully expecting to see a security guard in a cap with a set of handcuffs. But all there is is a fat man waving his arm because Kel's knocked his newspaper out his hand.

And as I turn back I let out a noise, a tiny sound that says *it's not true*. Only it is. I've done it. We've done it. And then I'm running, my feet pounding and my heart hammering and my head a mess of joy and victory and Oh My—

"GOD," yells Ang when they catch up. "That was slick, innit."

"Totally," pants Kel. "But seriously I'm going to do it in my knickers if we don't find a toilet."

"Drip drip drop," sings Ang.

"Nooooo!" protests Kel.

And then we've linked arms and we're making a run for Burger King over the road and everyone ducks out of our way 'cause they know we're queens right now, we rule.

And we rule all the way from Burger King past the tube to the bus stop and onto the back seat of the number twelve. That's when I hear someone say my name like they're not sure it's me, and I look up and there's Otis in his uniform and his hat and his face like a question mark.

Then the crowns fall.

McCardle calls it a fly in the ointment. Like in a story it can't all be happiness, something bad has to happen. Not big at first, just the first seed of rot, like a dot of mould on a slice of bread then, before you know it, the whole slice is covered in green and the world's gone upside down and broken apart.

Otis is my fly, I think, and my cheeks go hot like Kel's swiped them in blusher and I feel the buzz sink away and the food and fear churning in me and the eyeliner in my pocket burning like a glowstick that I'm sure he can see.

"Who's this then, your boyfriend?" says Ang, nudging Kel.

"I–it's—"

"Otis," he finishes for me. "And who might you fine young ladies be?"

Kel giggles and tells him her name.

"And what about you, angel?" says Otis.

"Oh my god. That *is* her name," says Kel. "She's Angel, innit."

"Well what else could she be," says Otis and he smiles so we can see his gold teeth and Kel smiles so he can see her black one and I smile even though I'm not doing that inside, not even close.

But Angel's not smiling, she's staring. "You her dad then?" she asks.

"No, he's my grandpa," I say quick.

"Step-grandpa, really," says Otis. "And the conductor of this fine vehicle so I got to go check for ragamuffins and daredevils downstairs. You girls behave like the ladies I know you are now," he says, bowing like we really are ladies.

"We will," I say.

And part of me wants to be a lady. Part of me wants to get rid of the eyeliner and Kel's stupid green nail varnish and Ang's lipstick that's going to make her look too old and too up for it. I want to be the girl Otis wants me to be, reckons we all can be, if we try.

But I can't be, not with Angel at my shoulder.

"Bus conductor, huh? Your mum must love that,"

she says, drawing out the "love" so I know she means the opposite.

"So what?" says Kel. "My grandpa was a driver, innit."

"Yeah, but your mum's not a flaming barrister is she," says Angel. "The only time she gets to court is when one of your uncles is in the dock."

"Piss off, Ang." Kel's genuinely annoyed now. And I want to say "piss off" again, too, but I can't rock the boat that much.

"Whatever," says Ang. "It's not like I'm lying."

"For once," says Kel.

"What's your problem?" says Ang. "Why've you gone and got the hump all of a sudden?"

"I haven't," says Kel. "Just, you know, respect and that."

"You sound like McCardle," says Ang. "That's chess club for you. You've gone all geek."

"Whatever," says Kel. But I know it's not whatever, it's something. It matters. Chess club matters 'cause her and Marvin are having a laugh and

171

Bloater's been off her case for a bit and all since she started winning so much.

And I could say this too, but all I can think is, if they're arguing about chess, they're not thinking about me and Mum, so I stay quiet and small in my seat and wish for Otis to stay downstairs and for the bus to get back to Peckham 'cause I want to get off.

Only when we do, I think I should've stayed on and gone all the way up Dulwich, or got off down Camberwell and said I needed the walk like I'm Mrs Joyful King and her fat legs, 'cause that's when I work out that Otis isn't the fly in this story at all. The fly is sat on a bench at the library bus stop watching everyone coming off the buses like he's waiting for his long lost mum to show up back from Benidorm.

The fly is Joe.

Fourteen

Don't see me, I think, and I try to squish myself behind Angel as we clump down the stairs and onto the pavement, but she's too thin and he's too quick and he's up and over to us before I can even think of an excuse.

"Where've you been?" he asks.

Angel's got *who the hell are you?* written all over her face but I'm not going to answer that, nor him. If I don't say anything then I can't lie any more or get into any more trouble.

But Joe's not going to shut up. "Thought you said your Mum was bad?"

"I . . ." I begin. But more words won't come.

"I came to see you, didn't I. I came to help."

"You went to the flat?" The words pop out 'cause I'm scared now. Of what he saw and what he's going to say and what Angel's going to say when he's done.

He nods. "She's not so bad, Ash. She's up and she made me tea and all."

My belly lurches like I'm still on the bus and we went over a hump.

"Why'd you lie?" he asks, straight out like that.

Then Kel's joining in. "Lie about what?"

"Nothing," I say. "It's not important."

"Yeah," says Joe, his voice quiet now. "Like me and all."

And I think Angel's going to ask her question now and I'm thinking fast about who I can say he is only it turns out she's not so bad at maths after all, 'cause she's worked it out already. "I know you," she says, deadpan, like she's still working out the details.

Joe says nothing.

"You're that kid who got Fletcher expelled," she carries on.

"What?" asks Kel.

"He—" I try to answer Kel, but Angel's not letting me get a word in.

"You're the one whose mum went off, innit."

Joe doesn't say yes or no. But he shrugs, which is all she needs. And I wait for it. The time bomb tick-tocking down the seconds as she puts all the pieces of the puzzle together, then *BAM*, she gets it, and my life explodes.

"You're— Shit, you're the one that put Mickey Dooley inside. Kel, he got your uncle banged up. It's him."

Kel's confused and Joe's saying nothing and I don't know what to say even if I could. Not that Angel would listen. She's on a roll, like she's Daphne from the Scooby gang solving the mystery and this bit is when she's pulling the mask off the monster and it

175

was the quiet kid all along. He's the baddie. Only he's not. He's . . .

"Joe," says Angel. "That's it. Joe Holt. I remember you from the paper. You were in our school, hung around with that Bradley kid."

"So?" he says.

"Kel, ain't you got nothing to say?"

But she hasn't, she's just biting her lip, like she don't know who to believe or what to do next.

Then Ang adds something else to the equation. "Is he . . . Oh my *god*. Is he your boyfriend, Asha?"

The cat lets go of my tongue. "No!" I blurt. Then quieter. "No, he's not. He's . . . He used to live near Otis. That's all. He's just . . . Joe."

Joe got that look again. Like I've slapped him with my words. "Thanks," he says. "That's who I am, is it? *Just Joe.* That's all?"

And I don't know what to say to that. Which way to go – if I say no, then Angel's going to think Christmas has come early, but if I say yes . . . I think of something Otis says, then. About being trapped.

I'm caught between the devil and the deep blue sea, I think. I don't want to hurt him. Joe don't deserve that. But if I don't, then I get hurt, don't I. And it's not like he *is* my boyfriend.

Not if Ang gets her way anyway.

"In that case he won't care you kissed Ronan Dooley then, will he."

I shake my head at Joe, willing him to not to rise to it, but he does.

"You kissed . . ." But he can't finish the sentence, can't say that name.

It was a dare, I want to say. *Just a dare.* But Ang's looking at me, eyebrow raised, smile on her like she won the flaming lottery. So it's my turn to just shrug.

He looks down at the ground. Like there's something fascinating on the pavement instead of just old, grey gum and spit.

"I read that book," he says. "The Ponyboy one. I got it out the library at school. You know what it's really about? What it's actually saying? Not that you should stick with your mates. I reckon it's saying that gangs are dumb. Gangs just get you in trouble. No one's better than anyone else. They just like to act it. Remember what Ponyboy says to that girl? That they watch the same sunset, or something like that."

I do remember. I remember Ponyboy saying it to that Soc, Cherry Valance. He meant they're not so different. No one is, underneath it all. And as I think that, I feel salt water sting my eyes and have to swallow the lump that rises in my throat. But even though I feel everything, I still say nothing. I can't. Cat really has got my tongue this time and I don't even think I want it back.

"Whatever," he says then. "See you."

"Wouldn't want to be you," says Ang to his back as he walks off. "Freak. What's he on about with all that sunset crap?"

I want to shout after him that I'm sorry for lying about my mum and I'm sorry for kissing Ronan Dooley and I'm sorry for everything but in the end all that comes out is, "That's the wrong direction for the bus, Joe." But he don't even look back, just carries on like he'd walk a hundred miles if it meant getting away from me.

And when I turn back Kelly's staring at me, her eyes cold and hard, Angel's arm through hers, marking her territory.

"You got some nerve," Kelly says, quietly. "Hanging about with me and saying nothing."

"I didn't know," I say. "Not for definite."

"What, with a surname like mine?"

I shrug again.

Angel laughs, shakes her head. "You owe her big time," she says.

I nod. "Like what?" I say. And right then I know I'll do anything, anything to get her and Angel back on side.

"We'll think of something," says Angel. "You'll see."

And then they're gone, down the High Street. I look at Angel, her hair swishing and her hips swinging, and I realise that I wasn't queen at all, not even for a minute. She was, and still is, and always will be. And, even though I'm surrounded by buses and cars and people in a giant swirling human soup, I've never felt more alone. I've lost Joe and Kel and maybe Angel too. I lost Patience days ago. That leaves Mum and Otis. And Mum was never on my side that much to begin with and Otis has gone off me since the party, so, after what Joe's done, I'm pretty sure I'm down to a big fat zero.

I feel sick as I walk up the stairs past Mrs Joyful King's and the Patels' and the Polish men's, sicker as I turn the key in the door, and by the time I'm standing in the front room I think I'm going to do it, that I'm going to hurl and I check for the bucket Mum's got just in case.

But she don't need the bucket today. She's not lying down. Joe was right, she's not bad, she's up. And she's sat at the table with a scarf on her bald head. And she's waiting for me.

"You home then."

I nod.

180

"You lied to that boy?" she says.

"I didn't want to hurt him," I say.

"Well you did," she says.

"You don't even like him," I say, and that's the truth. She can't even say his name.

"When have I said that?" she says.

"You don't have to say it," I say. " I see it."

"No, maybe I didn't at first," she says, nodding. "But Otis is right, he's a good boy. Better than girls who make you tell tales and lord knows what else."

I feel the eyeliner digging into my thigh and my stomach jumps again.

"I knew you wouldn't understand," I say. "Joe neither. That's why I didn't say nothing."

"*Anything*," she snaps back. "It's *say anything*."

And I feel my mouth set hard. 'Cause I'm tired of it. McCardle's always saying words matter and that we should use them wise and well. But they're just words in the end. It's deeds that do more, and I know mine haven't been great but nor have hers. Not really. And I know it's not her fault 'cause she didn't want to go get cancer or for Ellis to leave but all she can hear is me getting my words wrong – saying them like I'm Angel or Kelly or anyone from round here, all she can see is the bad stuff in people: the mistakes, the no money, the too much of it spent wrong.

"Whatever," I say.

And I don't listen when she starts on what that word even means, I just walk out the room, go into the bathroom and cry as quietly as I can. Then, when I'm done, I wash my face, go to my room, push the eyeliner to the back of my knicker drawer and curl up on the bed holding my stomach in one hand, my book in the other, and my heart in my head 'cause I know no one else is looking after it right now.

Fifteen

Otis gets me up Sunday.

I'm lying in bed, the book still unopened in my hand, and the smell of eggs coming through the door. I know she's told him 'cause I heard them before I went to sleep: whispering, teeth sucking, then her saying, "Leave it."

But he's not leaving it now. He pulls the curtain back so the light makes me squint. "Up, up," he says. "And put your glad rags on."

I don't get it. "What for?" I say, pulling the duvet

back over my head so I can't see him and the light can't see me.

"Breakfast," he says. "Then church."

I haven't been to church since I was little. Mum didn't have time; Sundays were all about prepping cases for her and homework for me and so God got put on a high-up shelf where we forgot about him. Until today.

I know why she's doing it. I read it in a magazine. When people nearly die they find religion and get all born again. 'Cause they're thankful. Or desperate maybe. We all do it a bit. Say a prayer when there's nothing left to lose. And, like I say, I don't even reckon I believe in him, least not that he's a man with a beard who lives in the clouds, nor that it's a woman like this girl Solace Lott reckoned, Mother Nature ruling us from up high and shaking her head when we leave the lights on. Only now, wedged in in the third pew from the front between Otis in his suit and Mum in her stupid wig, with Mrs Joyful

King's hat in the way and Patience refusing to turn round and look at me, I can feel him.

I can feel his eyes on me, feel him judging me. And when Reverend Williams talks about love and betrayal and tells the story of Judas I know it's me he's talking to. Only I don't want to listen and I fidget in my seat 'cause my skirt's itchy and my collar's tight and it's too hot.

Otis puts his hand on my knee. "Soon done," he says.

I look over at Patience again, willing her to turn round but her eyes are on her dad and her smile is wide and she's nodding like she knows every word is gospel truth. And I wonder why I can't do the same. Only then I think, I bet God never met Angel Jones. Then he'd have a hard time keeping out of trouble.

When the sermon's done; when the collection plate is piled with pound coins and fivers dug up like miracles from pockets and purses; when we've all finished bothering God with singing and praying and

185

saying his name, that's when the big scene starts. We're outside standing between the graves, with dead people under our feet wondering what the racket is, and it's like that story in the Bible and Mum's the Prodigal Son. They're all squeezing her arm and patting her and saying how good it is to see her, how good she looks, which is a fat lie and God knows it. She looks tired and thin and her clothes don't fit her any more and the wig's gone wonky so her head's lopsided and like a lollipop. I want to shrink then, disappear into myself, only they're hugging me too; women I don't remember with their arms so tight round me all I can smell is cheap perfume and I'm choking on that and their boobs squished in my face.

Only then I look up from Mrs Joyful King's lavender jacket and my heart and lungs stop dead. 'Cause that's when I see her – Kelly – sitting on the wall over the road eating a McMuffin and smoking a Marlboro Light and eyeing me like I'm the devil himself all done up in his Sunday best. Although I don't even think the devil would dare to wear yellow frills and a flaming daisy headband, unless he's, like, five years old.

I look away quick, pretend I'm interested in Mrs Joyful King's news about her son who's got a new job and she hopes he'll keep this one and stay on the right tracks this time away from them bad boys. And I'm looking all eager like a dog or like Patience in the pews, but inside I'm saying a prayer to that God who's got his beady eyes on me, 'cause I'm desperate now, 'cause I don't know what else to do. I ask him to make her go away, before she can see Mum can't walk without leaning on Otis like an old lady, before she says I'm a bitch or a traitor or a loser and tell me Monday morning, when I walk through the gates, I'm dead or as good as. But God's got other stuff on his mind 'cause as we turn to go she's still there, smoking and staring like she's lost a penny and found a tenner there on the pavement. And the tenner is me.

We start the walk up Choumert Road, and I don't

look round but I know she's following us. I can hear her footsteps and the *pant pant* of her dog who's had too many pasties for his tea. And when we walk up the stairs to the flat and I look out the window I see her again, on the wall where Patience used to wait, clocking the house, seeing it's just flats and ramshackle ones at that. Seeing how I live now. And I wonder how long I got before she tells Angel. And Angel gets her own back.

Midday, I chop carrots for Otis and peel potatoes and don't pull a face when he yanks out the guts from a fish that's got its eyeballs still in.

One o'clock I set the table and pour water into one glass and squash in another and Guinness into the last topped up with condensed milk, Otis's favourite.

Two o'clock we sit at the table and Mum eats her food and drinks her water and lets Otis pour some of his sweet stout for her, and she does pull a face but she still drinks it down 'cause he says it's good for her and I think it's weird that she used to be a child, spoon- and bottle-fed at this table, and she's a child again now and Otis is the daddy.

Three o'clock I get my books out and she looks at the marks on my work and sucks her teeth 'cause I got a B, and I wonder what Angel's mum thinks when she gets her Cs and if she shouts or throws a party and I bet myself it's the last one, but I keep it to myself 'cause I owe Mum, I owe everyone.

And four o'clock Angel calls it in.

The text says, *Come round Kels now.*

I feel weightless then, like I'm at the very top of the loop-the-loop and gravity is gone for a split second, before I'm plunging, the speed of it pulling me down and I'm heavy as a ten-tonne elephant hitting the floor. And I want to get off, I want to. But I can't. I got to do this. I got to face up to it and let her hit me with her best shot even if that's kissing some cousin or nicking a pen or drinking 'til I'm sick. It's honour. It's what you do when you're in a gang. You stick together.

I read it again. *Come round Kels now.* And I hear my mum putting the apostrophe in and I hate her and I hate me for thinking it, but I got to be sweet as the Guinness drink so I smile and say I got to pop out, I need Tippex for my homework. And Mum looks like she can't decide whether to be cross I made a mistake or wonder if I'm lying, but Otis he just says to get him some chocolate spread for toast later and gives me two pounds. So in less than five minutes since Angel texted, and five hours since she started plotting, I'm out the door, walking steady one-two, one-two, then faster one-two-one-two-one-two until both feet leave the ground and I'm running hard and fast, round the corner, past the scrappy piece of grass that counts as a park, and the corner shop that's open all hours only it shut two years ago, and then there I am, on the doorstep of 13 Ephraim Street along with a broken cooker and a bag of dog poo.

Kelly's mum answers and I can tell she doesn't know, that Kel's not said about Joe, 'cause she gives me a smoke-fuggy hug and sends me upstairs with three Cokes and half a packet of pink wafers. The bedroom door's shut when I get up though and I wonder whether I should knock or just go in, which will annoy them less? And I'm standing there with Liam in his no-nappy begging me for a biscuit when I hear her. Angel.

"What are you waiting for? Flipping Christmas?"

"Here," I say to Liam and put a pink wafer in his sticky fingers and he gives me a smile so wide I wish I could stay out here on the landing for a bit, for ever, with the kitchen radio playing pop music and Mrs Dooley singing along and the dogs on their backs down in the hallway waiting for someone to notice them. And I must be there too long 'cause then the door opens and a hand grabs my arm and yanks me inside.

Kel. Course, it's Kel, 'cause Angel's bagged the best seat on the top bunk, and Kel squeezes into the bottom one with all of Sharon's bears and rabbits like a nylon zoo so I got nowhere to sit but the floor.

"You want a Coke?" I ask, but they've both got chocolate Yazoo and Angel throws me a look like I'm an idiot for even asking, so I put them on the floor next to me with the biscuits and I try not to think about the last time I was sat there, when Ronan Dooley had his mouth on mine and his hands where he shouldn't.

"So that was some lie you pulled," she says.

"I …" I begin. But I can't find the right words, lost for them. 'Cause how do you start to explain that your mum ain't no bigshot anymore and, oh yeah, she nearly died – might still – and you didn't tell no one, not even your so-called best friends.

Angel got words though. She's always got words. Only not the ones I expect. "Some big stunt, that. Keeping him secret from Kel and her secret from him and all. Think you're some double agent, do you?"

I shake my head slowly, as I slowly get it. She don't know about Mum. If she did she'd be all over it. I flick a glance at Kel but she looks away quick. *Thank you*, I say silent-like, trying to transfer thoughts from my head into hers. It's called telepathy; I read about it in a magazine and it's totally true. Only Kel don't seem to hear me 'cause she still won't meet my eye.

"So, you made it up with him yet? That retard?" Angel says.

"He's not . . ." I begin. Not my boyfriend, not a retard. But she don't want to hear it. Don't care. So I just shake my head instead. "Not answering my texts," I say. And that's the truth. I tried ten times, twenty even. But nothing, and when I call him it goes straight to voicemail.

"So we worked out what you got to do to make it up to us," says Angel. "Haven't we, Kel?"

Kel's still saying nothing, just nods. Only Ang can't hear a nod, can she.

"Oi, Kel."

"All right," Kel says, "I can hear you." Then to me, quieter, "Yeah, we did."

I wait while Ang does her Simon Cowell dramatic pause. One, two, three . . .

"Black Dare," she says, and I hear the audience she

wishes was there gasp while I stand like a fool in the spotlight.

"I— What's that?" I say.

"Same as a dare," says Angel. "Only you can't call truth, you can't call chicken. Whatever we say, you just got to do it."

"But that's . . ." My brain's whirring and whizzing with it, with the terrible possibility of it. "What if you said to kill myself. Or to kill, I don't know, Darryl Benson?"

"As if," says Angel. "Like I give a shit about him."

"It's McCardle," blurts out Kel.

"You want me to kill McCardle?"

"You read too many books, Ash," says Angel. "Why would I do that? He might be a dick but I'm not going to get him killed, am I. Just . . . riled. I mean, really really riled."

Riled isn't dead. But it's not good, for him or for me, and I'm glad I'm sitting down 'cause my blood's all rushed to my head and I know my legs couldn't keep me up.

"How?" I ask.

Angel snorts. "I don't know. Up to you. You're always off with him in some corner so it can't be that hard."

"I'm not," I say.

"Whatever. You want to watch yourself, though. You know he got previous."

"What d'you mean?"

"You don't know his story?" Angel looks like she's got the secret of the Arc of the Covenant ready to burst out of her.

I shake my head.

"He was in a gang," Ang says. "One of Kel's cousins knew him when they was kids, didn't he, Kel."

Kel nods but Angel don't wait to hear a reply this time. "Got done for robbing some phone shop with a knife, only when he was inside they put him on this scheme and he got all his exams and now he's preaching to all of us like he's Jesus flaming Christ only we know where he come from, don't we."

So he does have a story. A story like Ponyboy's, with gangs and rumbles and knives. A story so big it could be a film down the Premier, with that bloke who plays Luther in the lead.

But I've read the book. And this isn't the way the story's supposed to end.

"But he wouldn't ... he wouldn't hurt anyone now," I say.

"I reckon he would. Reckon he still got it in him," says Angel. "Like them dogs that are trained to fight. Even when they're rescued they have to put them down in the end, 'cause if anything snaps at them they lose it."

I still don't get it. "But why?" I say. "What's he done to you?"

"Nothing," she says. "Everything."

And then I understand. That's it, what she's so angry about. That he does nothing. He ignores her. She doesn't exist for him except as an annoyance. A fly buzzing around his head and he's just swatting it away lazily.

And I'm right.

"All he cares about is you," she continues. "You and Patience and Kelley flaming Eckersley."

"That's bullshit—" I begin.

"Bull true," she says. "Not me he asked to go to writing club, is it. Not me who gets his precious book— Oh, hang on." She's onto something now, found her treasure. "That's it!" she says. "That's what you go to do. You got to kill the book."

My stomach drops like it's got lead in it, not lunch. "What?" I say.

"Yeah," she carries on, loving her own idea, lit up by it. "You got to drown it or burn it or— Or pull it apart page by page."

"But that book's like, I don't know, like a talisman or something. You can't," I say. "You can't do that to him."

"But I'm not," she smiles. "I'm not doing it to him. You are."

I let the words hang in the air for a minute, flashing my fate in invisible neon.

"And if I don't do it," I say, eventually. "Then what?"

"Easy," she says. "Then we tell everyone about how you're a liar, and a slut, and how you and that mental boyfriend of yours stitched up Kel's uncle."

I look over at Kel, 'cause I want to say sorry and ask her to forgive me, like Reverend Williams says God does, even if you do the worst thing possible, but she's not God, she's just Kel, fiddling with the duvet cover. Angel's the one in charge. And she's not interested in *sorry*s or *please*s. She's more an eye for an eye.

There's only one question left.

"When?" I ask.

"Friday," she says. "You got 'til Friday."

My head's so messed with it on the way home I don't even try to text Joe again. And I forget to get Tippex or Nutella and have to go back to the shop as soon as I get in, 'cause Otis's giving me a look like I'm on my last chance, so I say I bumped into

Patience and got distracted 'cause I figure the way I'm heading one more lie can't hurt me.

I go to bed early and all; say I'm not feeling great and it's not even a lie 'cause my stomach's flip-flopping and my head feels full of dust instead of brains. But I don't sleep. I just lie there, with the book in my hands, wondering what I got myself into, and what I'm going to do now.

I think about Ponyboy and Sodapop and Johnnycake. I think about what Joe said about gangs being dumb. But then I think, too, about how they all only got each other, that's why they got to stick together. And what Angel said's true – that McCardle don't let her do anything; he's written her off before she's even had a chance to prove him wrong, or right. So she cheeks a lot and sasses but it don't make her the baddie, not really. And then I know I got to do it. I got to prove to her that I believe in her, and Kel and all. That we're the same, me and them. Got messed up family and stories to tell, just maybe not the ones McCardle likes to hear.

So now that's settled, I got to work out how to do it. How to make him mad. I can't trash the book and hand it back to him. He might forgive me, mightn't he, the big man he is. No, I got to build up to it. Got to make him believe I'd do it deliberate, like Ang might. Got to make up a story.

So I think about things I've seen and read. I think about stories with heroes who turn out to be villains all along. I think about what McCardle said: that the real baddies arrive as your friend. They say what you want to hear so you trust them, so you like them. But then they stick the knife in.

Then I get it, it pings into my head; a giant light bulb shining on all the shit that's going on, lighting up the dust so I can see that it's not empty in there after all, there's a gleaming gem in the corner. Because I've remembered something I read in a magazine once, about this woman called Deborah whose boyfriend used to go mental every time she sang Dolly Parton songs and she rigged up a camera and sang "Jolene" so she could catch him losing it.

So then I know what I got to do: I got to find his "Jolene" – that way he's already angry with me when I hand over the book; the book will be the final straw.

That's all I got to do. I got to find his "Jolene".

Sixteen

It's easy when you think about it, obvious even. 'Cause what he hates isn't Angel cheeking or Kelly swearing or Bradley and his mates chucking pens about. It's not even when Darryl Benson thinks Dracula and Frankenstein are mates and McCardle has to explain for the tenth time that Frankenstein made the monster, he wasn't one himself. What gets him isn't getting it wrong; it's not even trying. It isn't being bad at words; it's not caring about them. It's not not having talent; it's wasting it, tipping it down the drain like flat Coke. So in English on Tuesday I start tipping mine, a loud, steady *drip-drip-drip*, the kind of noise you try to block out but even if you stick your fingers in your ears or hum the national anthem it's there in the background driving you mental.

First off I haven't got my homework, and I don't have an excuse like I lost it or the computer crashed or even a dog ate it. I just haven't done it. And I don't even say I thought it was for next week like this kid Harvey does. I just shrug and say I was watching *The X Factor* final on telly, innit, and as the words come stumbling out my mouth I think that maybe I'm going to be sick and all but I keep it in, I swallow and take this massive breath and raise my eyebrow like Angel does and wait for him to lose it.

"What about Sunday? You had a whole day then," he says.

"God's day. No one's supposed to work on Sunday," I say. Even though I know Patience must've spent half the afternoon in her bedroom writing the eight pages she's come up with.

"She's right," says Angel. "It's against religion."

"And which religion would that be in your case, Angel?" asks McCardle.

"Like that's your business," she snaps back. "I might be Muslim, innit."

"Lying's against Islam," says Jordan O'Keefe, whose mum's going out with Mr Hassan from Hassan's Deals on Rye Lane.

"Oh, piss off, Muhammed," says Angel.

"So you're Muslim now?" McCardle looks at me.

"I never said that," I smirk. "C of E, innit. I went to church. Patience'll tell you." And I look over at her but she's got her eyes on McCardle like he's the preacher now and I'm the sinner in the pews.

"I don't need witnesses," says McCardle. "I need your homework. In by Friday or you'll be in detention."

And then I give him the cherry on the top. "Whatever," I say.

Angel snorts and Kel coughs so hard I think she's going to spit out the gum he hasn't seen yet but I just keep my eyes on him, willing him, daring him to do something. And even though all that happens is that he tells us to pick up our books and turn to page eighty-nine, I know it worked. Because it takes him a second too long before he looks away, and that means I got to him. I read it in a magazine.

Angel knows it too.

"Nice start, Ash," she says as she walks past me at my locker.

And I should feel that thrill, that joy that I'm getting back on the ride with her. But, as I watch her and Kel, waltzing arm in arm down the corridor, their skirts rolled up and their high ponytails swinging, I realise the buzz has gone. Now it's just something I've got to do. And I got three more days to do it.

Wednesday I sow more seeds. It's not so easy this time 'cause I haven't got Angel and Kel with me, backing me up with their bitching and their boredom. No, this time it's writing group and I got the hands-up me-sir lot. I got Kelley Eckersley with Seamus's scarf round her neck like it's Harry Potter's cloak of flaming invisibility. I got Patience with her pages of poems that drip smugness along with God's love. I got Dennis who's only got eyes for Patience though she's twice his size and half as good looking. And I hear Angel in my head as I think all this, hear her saying the mean words and I wonder how much of her is me now, and where Ash has gone, and if I even want her back. And hearing her voice makes it OK somehow when I do it. Like it's not me who laughs at Kelley's story about falling in love down the dog track.

"That where you met Seamus?" scoffs the not-me. "Which one of you's the dog?"

"That's enough," snaps McCardle.

And it's not-me who rolls her eyes at him, who *whatever*s him under her breath.

It's not-me who yawns when Patience is talking about parables and how we should all write a book of new parables, set in Peckham.

"Gripping," says not-me. "Loaves and flaming fishes."

"Leave her alone," says Kelley. "I like it."

"You would. Every one knows you're the Good Samaritan. Taking Seamus back even after he's had his hands up Chelsea's skirt."

"Asha, outside, now," fires McCardle. "Bring your things."

And the girl that's me sighs, like it's all such a drama, picks up her paper and pens, pulls her bag onto her shoulder, and follows him into the corridor.

"What's going on?" he asks, and even though it's only three words, I can hear the swearing that's shouting out in his head, can see it dancing behind the blacks of his eyes.

"Nothing," says the girl.

"Asha." He shakes his head. "I asked you to join this group because I thought you had it in you. I thought we understood each other."

The new me feels a twinge of something, like a needle in her side, rooting around, digging for the

207

old Asha underneath. Telling me I'm worth more than this. That I'm like him. Saying the same stuff that Joe does – that Ponyboy does – the same kindness that feels like syrup.

But the new me ignores it, spits it out, remembers that he don't think Angel's worth nothing, nor Kel. The new me sticks her fingernails into her palms as a distraction. "You thought wrong," she says.

"No one's forcing you to be here," he says finally.

"Then I'll be seeing you," says new me.

"Don't do this to yourself," he says.

"I'm not," says new me. "I'm doing it to you."

"It might feel like it," he says. "But it's only you you're screwing in the end."

"You even allowed to say that word?" says new me. "I could do you for that."

"You're making a mistake," he says.

New Asha shoots a look through the criss-crossed glass of the classroom door, sees the faces staring at her, wondering, wanting to know what's happening.

"No, you are," she says, all quiet.

And the new me walks down the dirty tiles of the corridor, through the double doors, and out into the sunshine of the street, and she doesn't once look back.

"You're home early," says Mum. "Thought you had writing group."

"McCardle got funny," I say. "Shouted at me. Swore and all."

Mum sucks her teeth. "That school," she says. "I knew it."

And another seed is sown.

Thursday I do it. I ruin the book. And I'm not going to lie, it hurts. It don't feel right, ripping pages out, dripping nail varnish on the cover. Like spitting on the truth or something. But I do it anyway, 'cause I know I got to. And something weird happens, 'cause part of me – the new me – feels good when it's done. And I know then that's how Angel feels when she's done something crazy. It's power, innit. It's being somebody, somebody who gets noticed. And I am so going to get noticed for this. This is my last seed. The last straw.

So come Friday it's all there, like kindling stacked for a fire, waiting for me to light it: the row in class, the fight in the corridor. All I got to do is not hand in my homework, get hauled in for detention at lunch, then hand him the book instead. Then it's done. Then it's over.

Isn't it?

Seventeen

When I think of all the people I ever wanted to be, I'm pretty sure this isn't one of them.

I wanted to be Emily Davison, throwing myself in front of the King's horse so I can change the world. I wanted to be Michelle Obama, only with me in the President's chair not my husband. I wanted to be Angelina Jolie, beautiful and clever with all them multi-coloured kids showing I'm kind and all. But I'm none of them. I'm not even Hannah Montana, playing at being two girls in two worlds. 'Cause both of those girls are cool, or they were, back when I was eight anyway.

I don't really know who I am anymore, so much of me is lies and games and bits of other people. Half of me wants to bottle it. Wants to turn around, and run, feet slapping, heart pounding, back to the flat, tell Mum I can't do it any more, that she needs to get me out of that school, get me into Haberdashers', or anywhere, anywhere but here.

But that new part of me thinks McCardle got it coming, lording it up, pretending to be king of the school when he's just a kid from Peckham. And that's the part that nods when Angel pulls me over in the playground, says, "You got 'til the end of the day, yeah? Then I'm calling it in."

That's the part that turns up late to second period so he's already on my case before I sit down. That's the half that leans back in her chair and shrugs when he says, "Aren't you forgetting something?"

I walk to his desk, wait a few seconds, scratch my head, pat my pockets, giving it the big I-am, then say, "You're right, sir, I left my phone at home. Now how am I going to play Angry Birds at lunch?"

The audience cheers and jeers.

"Settle down," McCardle says, waving his hands like he's damping down flames.

I turn and take a bow.

"I assume by your newfound ambition to play the fool that you haven't managed to do your homework."

"Never assume, sir. It makes an ass of you and me."

Kelly lets out a whoop.

"That's enough from you too, Dooley. Or I'll see you at lunch."

"Ooooo," yells Angel. "Taking your students for lunch. Isn't that illegal at your age, sir?"

The class is going mental, and I'm stood in the middle of it, watching it all, watching McCardle's face tighten and his hands clench into the fists I know he wants to aim at me.

"McCardle and Dooley up a tree, K-I-S-S-I-N-G," sings Angel.

And that's it. That's all it takes in the end. A stupid playground song.

"Enough!" His hand slams down on the desk, sending pens scattering and clattering onto the floor.

The room's silent, then, and still. I can see Patience looking at a biro rolling across the lino, wanting to pick it up for him like the teacher's pet she is, but not even she dares risk it. And even though it's not me he's hit, there's the thought in their heads now that he could do it, that he's mad at me. And that's all I need. That and the set-up. And he hands it to me on a plate.

"Wright, Dooley, Jones. Back here at lunch. And the rest of you had better settle if you don't want to join them."

But I pray really hard and this time God's got nothing better to do, so in the end he grants my prayer and it's just the three of us that walk out with a detention set for one o'clock. And just the three of us that sit down in that room with the world shut out behind a door and only McCardle to defend himself.

*

He's got a speech all worked out. A heartbreaking plea for mercy.

"I know what you're doing," he says. "But it won't work. I'm not that kid anymore. And you – none of you – have to be either. You have a chance here. That's what school is, a chance to be better than people think you are, than *you* think you are. And you're wasting it. I thought you were different, Asha. But you're letting them bring you down." And he shakes his head like he's sad, not angry now.

"Thanks a lot," says Angel. "Nice to know you care."

"I'd care if you did," he says. "But you don't. Or you won't."

Angel sucks her teeth, stares out the window. Kelly looks over at me like she's waiting for something and I can't tell if it's a fight or surrender.

But I'm not backing down, not now I got this far. I look at him sat there all calm now, thinking we're all useless, all three of us, and at that second I hate him, I really do. And that's when I do it, I pull my rabbit out of the hat.

"Oh, I forgot something," I say. "Thanks for the lend, but it's not really my thing after all." And I chuck the devastated, desecrated book across so it lands with a thump on the desk in front of him.

He looks at it, not touching it, but not understanding either. Then slowly, slowly he picks it up, turns it over, sees what's underneath the pink-polish drips, sees the missing pages, the ruined story. And then – kerching! – the penny drops and the next thing I know he's standing over my desk and raging at me so hard I see the whites of his eyes and the gold of his tooth and feel the little flecks of spit hit my cheek as he tells me who I am – and it ain't a "somebody", it's a big fat no one.

"Stand up," he rages.

And I'm scared, then. Proper scared. So I do, but something happens: I trip over the chair and pitch forward into him so that he has to push me back so's I stand upright.

And then I know I done it. I got my "Jolene". And more and all – more than I bargained for, more than even Angel wanted. So that when he says, "Headmaster, now," I don't argue, I walk straight out the door down the corridor to Hopkins' office before I can change my mind. And when I get there I tell the truth. I tell him that I messed up the book and McCardle got mad. But I do something else and all. I do a dare, bigger than the Black Dare, bigger than Angel asked for, because he deserved it, because he scared me, and because I know Hopkins is going to believe it. I dare myself, and that dare is that I tell him McCardle pushed me and Kelly Dooley and Angel Jones saw it all.

It all happens quick after that, like when you fast-forward a DVD. So swift I can't barely catch breath.

First Hopkins tells me this is a serious accusation and I had better have my facts straight if I want to make an official report.

"I do," I say. "I'm not making it up. You can ask

Angel and Kelly, sir. And anyone in English 'cause he shouted at me this morning and all. Hit the desk and everything. He's a liability, innit. Dangerous."

"I think someone else can be the judge of that," he says. "I'll have to call your mother, of course. She'll need to come in."

My legs, so solid until now, so sure of what they were doing, of what I was doing, shake in their wrong colour shoes. "What?" I say. "Why? When?"

"Well . . ." He looks at his watch. "It'll be Monday I should think."

I try to think of an excuse, conjure up a chemo appointment out of the thin, biscuit-smelling air in here, but even though my mouth's open, nothing comes out of it. Not a single word.

"You'd better go now," he says. "I'll call in the other two this afternoon, but in the meantime please don't talk about this to anyone. Things need . . ." He trails off, fiddles with his ugly brown tie. "They need to be bottomed out."

A month ago, a week ago, I'd have laughed at that

like I was Bradley flipping Spencer. But now I just nod like a moron instead. Like a robot, 'cause that's what I am now, doing what my control-panel-Angel tells me to do. Now I just think, "I got to talk to them before he does. I got to tell them to say he pushed me." And I got to get a bruise and all. And by the end of afternoon, our story's straight and Angel's made Kel smack me one on my BCG scar.

"Ow! Where'd you learn that?" I ask.

"My mam," she says. And I don't say anything after that, 'cause I got my own mum to worry about.

She knows before I even walk in the door. Hopkins has called her, or Miss Merritt has, in between redoing her gels.

"You're not going back," she says.

"I got to," I say. "Monday. I got to go in. We both got to."

"After that, then," she replies. "I knew this was a mistake."

And all I can think is, *She believes me. She believes in me.*

"How?" says Otis. "What you going to do, Chrissie? Teach her all her times tables yourself?"

Mum shakes her head, ignores him. "We'll find a way," she says to me. "You and me. Like we always do."

And I want to believe her. I want to believe it really is me and her against the world like two superheroes. Only one of us is bald and full of drugs and covered in scars, and one's a liar. And there's not much super about that, is there.

As I lie in bed that night, with my arm aching and my eyes sore from crying and my legs still shaking like I'm old Nanu Patel from downstairs, I don't feel brave or brilliant or any of the things I need to feel. I don't think I've done the dare, won the bet, beaten Angel at her own game.

All I think is, *What have you done, Ash? What the flip have you done?*

Eighteen

It's Kel who calls me, not the other way round. I remember that later, like I'm Sherlock. It's important.

It's Sunday night and I'm in my room where I've been nearly all weekend, ignoring Otis and his offers to take me on the bus up West, or up the park to see the parakeets.

"Can't stay in there forever, chile," he says. "Got to face the world."

Tomorrow, I think. I'll face it tomorrow. And I

wonder if somehow I can make sure tomorrow never comes, that I get stuck in this moment like in a film or a story, where everything's on repeat so I'd just keep waking up at 10.23 a.m. and eating Coco Pops in bed and wondering where the pink stain on my duvet came from. Maybe, if I got stuck, I think, I'd get the chance to do it all again, only this time I could do it right. And it's right when I'm thinking that that my phone goes.

"Kel?" I ask, even though I know it's her 'cause her name flashes up. Only it's weird 'cause it's never her that rings, it's always Angel, and she's not called for over a week.

"Yeah," she says. Then she's quiet for a bit before she asks, "You OK?"

"S'pose," I lie.

Then neither of us say anything and all I can hear is Katy Perry singing about being a tiger in the background and I know Kel's shut in the bathroom and Sharon's next door dancing in that pink bubble of a bedroom. Sometimes silence is loud. So thick you can slice it. In the end we both got a knife in our hands.

"I'm—" we both begin.

"You go first," she says.

"No, you," I say. 'Cause she called me.

Then she comes out with two words that are so far from what I'm expecting I have to say, "What?" like I'm deaf or an idiot.

"I'm sorry," she repeats.

It's my turn to be quiet for a bit 'cause I'm trying to work out what she's sorry for. If it's McCardle or the Ronan thing or smoking or drinking or just all of it, this whole mess I'm in – *we're* in – and if she's really sorry or if Angel's on her shoulder playing the devil again.

"She with you?" I ask in the end.

She doesn't need to ask who I'm talking about. "No," she says. "She's up town with her mum buying shoes. Fat Brian gave her some money, innit."

"I thought it was from her dad?" I say. "She said he sent it."

"She says a lot of stuff," says Kelly eventually.

And it's like she's dropped the worst swear ever then, because she never badmouths Angel, not when Angel calls her out for her family or her clothes or chess club. And then I see it, a chink of something in this blackness, like Kel's opened up a door and a sliver of hope has snuck in. But I can't tell her, can't ask her to be my partner in crime. Because that—that would be the biggest dare of all.

So I do what I should've done all the other times: I bottle it. "Thanks for calling," I say.

"*De nada*," she replies.

But it isn't nothing. It's a big fat something and we both know it.

"See you tomorrow, then," I say.

"Yeah, see you," she says. "Wouldn't want to be you."

I almost laugh. "Who would?" I say.

I don't go to school in the morning. Otis calls in sick for me and Hopkins says he understands in the circumstances but it can't be a habit and I shouldn't let my education suffer because of this, only Mum says my education's suffering if I *do* go in so I can't win. But I knew that before.

"You got to come later though," Otis says. "To the meeting."

I want the world to stop. I want the ground to open up and swallow me into a giant sinkhole like they get in Florida. I want winged monkeys to fly in through the window and carry me to Oz.

But this is Peckham, not telly.

"Who else?" I say.

"Me, your mum, the other two girls ... the teacher," finishes Otis.

My stomach turns and I wonder if I'm really sick, like if I throw up my piece of toast, he'll let me stay behind and Hopkins can do the whole thing without me, have a trial without a victim.

Only they don't, do they. 'Cause the victim's not me. And Otis, he knows it.

"You don't have to do this," he says.

"Do what?" says Mum.

"She know what I'm talking about."

I look at him, at his eyes like X-ray specs that see the truth in everything, see dull skin beneath glitter, and weakness behind fighting talk. But he can't see what I can: that it's not me who wants this, it's Angel and what she says is golden, is law. And Mum wants it too 'cause it makes her right all along, so right she's in her court suit, pinstriped and ironed, ready to make the case for the prosecution. Only the jacket hangs off her and her wig don't even look real for a second and that's when I wonder if Angel knows about Mum after all, and knew this would happen. That if I won the dare I'd have to bring her in so they could see.

"I do," I say. "I do have to do it." And Mum nods, and Otis drops his head and closes his all-seeing eyes and the truth is shut in its box with a snap.

The meeting's at one-thirty – lunchtime – so we have to go in with half the school staring like we're freaks or geeks or dead men walking. And whatever Hopkins told Angel or Kelly about keeping it quiet, they all know, or think they do.

"Did he really slap you?" says some girl in Year Ten I never spoke to before. "'Cause Stacey heard off Siobhan that he did and that you slapped him back."

"He wasn't in class today," says someone else. "We had Bloater instead so thanks a bunch."

"Don't listen," says Otis, putting his hand on my shoulder and hurrying me through, his other arm linked with Mum's.

She got her eyes fixed ahead, like she's scared if she looks down she'll see she's wading in dirt. She don't even nod when Patience gives her this small, neat smile from across the corridor. I don't smile back neither, 'cause my heart's going and I think if I can just get through the doors inside I'll be fine, the bullets will stop, only when we do I realise we've gone from the jungle into the tigers' den. 'Cause lined up on chairs outside Hopkins' office are Mrs Dooley, Mrs Jones, Angel and Kelly.

Mrs Dooley don't look up 'cause she's got Cheryl on her lap trying to unwrap a KitKat and she's wailing 'cause she's got chocolate on her fingers, but Mrs Jones stares at Mum the way I seen Angel stare at people: like she's gum on her shoe.

Otis nods at Mrs Jones but she don't nod back, just says, "I had to take an afternoon off work for this," then gives me a look like I'm worse than gum and she just stepped in me.

But even that's nothing compared to Angel's face. Only it's not me she's looking at, it's Mum. Staring at the wig. At the way she's been leaning on Otis. Listening to her breathing hard, like she's climbed Everest not walked round the corner. And I see Mum though Angel's eyes, see the sickness and the weakness. But I see something else too, I see that Mum's out the house, she fighting for me. Even if it's the wrong fight.

"I didn't know . . ." Angel trails off. And I believe her.

I look at Kelly. She don't say anything, but she does something that shouts louder than words. She

228

takes my hand, the one that's gripping the grey plastic of the chair, and squeezes it, just once, then drops it before Angel catches her.

"I see he's not shown his face then," says Mrs Jones. "McWotsit."

Mum looks at her then, at her orange skin and pink nails and yellow hair, none of it what God gave her. "He'll be seen separately," she says. "We all will. It's procedure." She looks away again like the sight of her turns her stomach. Only Mrs Jones isn't done yet.

"Surprised to see you here," she says. "Surprised to see you back if I'm honest."

Mum don't want to answer that one, so Otis does it for her. "We all surprised by life sometimes. But surprises not all bad."

"Tell that to Asha," says Mrs Jones. "Poor thing. Should've stayed away after all."

Otis got nothing to say to that and nor has anyone else and I'm almost glad when Hopkins opens the door so we can begin.

*

He sees us in turn, like Mum said, like on telly in those police shows. He's got to check our facts, make sure our stories match up, see if there's any holes in them.

Angel's first in, 'cause her mum's kicked off and said she's got to be back at work for stocktake, but it's more likely for Fat Brian. I nearly say "good luck" only that don't seem right and anyway she don't need luck, she says you make your own and I can tell by the way she walks in, chin up and hand on her hip, that she's got some today. When she comes out again five minutes later she's smiling as she drops into a chair.

"Easy," she says. "Knew it would be."

"What did you say?" asks Kel.

"The truth, I hope," says Otis, even though he knows she's not talking to him, not even caring he's there.

She nudges Kel to get her to laugh but Kel pulls away.

"Whatever," says Angel. "Enjoy."

And then she's gone, taking her smell of Chanel and her secrets with her.

It's me next. I thought it'd be Kel, but Hopkins comes out and nods at me and Mum.

"Asha? Mrs Wright? Mr . . ." He looks at a piece of paper. "I'm sorry, I . . ."

"Otis," says Otis, standing. "Just Otis is fine."

Hopkins looks put out, but he nods again, like a toy dog on a car dashboard. "Do come in then."

"Nearly over," says Otis, as he takes my arm.

But when I get inside I realise it's only just begun.

'Cause Mum got it wrong. McCardle's not coming later, he's already in there, the book in his hand like it's a smoking gun. And another woman too, one I don't know, her hair tight off her head like a cheap facelift and her lips even tighter.

"This is Miss Cooper from the LEA," says Hopkins. "And Mr Mc—"

"He shouldn't be here," interrupts Mum. "It's not right. It's intimidation."

"We thought—"

It's Miss Cooper's turn to interrupt. "*I* thought it might help matters, to hear both sides of the story, if Asha doesn't object."

"I ..." I begin. But I don't finish 'cause I'm thinking hard then, whether I do object or not, whether it's easier if I can see him, remind myself of the way his face got when he hit the desk, of how angry he was. Or whether it's easier to lie if he's out the room.

"I— It don't matter," I say. Then I correct myself before Mum does. "Doesn't."

"It does matter," Mum says, finding something else to pull me up on. She's het up now, sweat on her forehead 'cause she's cross and scared and it's hot in that wig.

But Otis puts his hand on her arm, pats it, like he's trying to calm an animal. "Maybe it for the best," he says. "More truth come out when you face up to it."

Mum bats his hand away. "What more truth is there?"

Otis looks at me then and my insides swirl and my skin turns so cold I shiver, a ghost walking down my spine. I turn away from his eyes, but truth is calling at me, saying my name everywhere I look: in Hopkins' hands folded on his desk, in Miss Cooper's fingers fiddling with her cheap-looking Argos ring, and most of all in McCardle. In every inch of him. The blackness of his eyes, the way his jaw's set tight, like if he let go for even a second he'd collapse, a puppet with its strings snipped.

"So you want to start, Asha?" says Hopkins.

I look at McCardle again, our eyes fixed on each other, like it's the playground and we're in a staring competition and neither of us is going to back down, the stakes are too high.

And they are. They're so high. Higher than I realised. So dizzying I feel like I might faint from it and I wonder if I should fake it anyway 'cause that might end it, they'd have to carry me out and give me smelling salts and biscuits and Mum would say, "It's too much for her," and they'd leave it at that.

Only they won't, will they. They won't drop it until I've said my story. Told my tale. I wonder what words Angel used. If she added stuff from what we agreed. If there's swearing or smacking or sobbing in her scene. Then I wonder what Kelly'll say, 'cause she don't talk that much, only if she has to. She didn't even say a word when she found out about me and Joe and her uncles.

And that's when I remember. I remember that *she* called *me*. Not me her. And I remember what she said and all. *She says a lot of stuff* – those were her words. And something happens in me – in my head and deeper down in my insides, something flickers and it's like those two things are gleaming gems in the dirt and dust, those things are truth and I'm seeing them with Otis's X-ray eyes now. And they add up to one simple fact: that Angel's not always right.

I know then what I have to say. And it's big and

scary and I have to dare myself again. But that's truth for you.

I'm still looking McCardle in the eye when I say it, so he can see it in me. "I lied," I say. "He didn't do it."

And McCardle lets his eyes fall, drops his head into his hands.

"Oh, chile," Otis says.

"W-what?" Mum's voice stutters like a broken engine.

"It's true. It was a dare. Angel put me up to it. I ruined the book – that book," I point to it, still in McCardle's hand. "I'm sorry," I say to him. "I'm so sorry. I did it so you'd get mad. She told me to. She was going to . . . she was going to do some stuff if I didn't."

He nods at me, like he gets it. *Oh God, please let him get it*, I think, and I hope Patience done enough praying for both of us so that if there is someone up there they hear this.

And then it comes out. All of it. Bunking off

school, going up West, stealing. I don't say about Seamus and Ronan, 'cause Mum's got too much to cope with without seeing that in her head, but I don't leave anything else out – not the eyeliner nor the Malibu nor the Dooleys nor the way I treated Patience and Joe. Hopkins looks confused then 'cause he can't remember who Joe is and it don't seem relevant only it is, all of it connects up. It all matters. And something else matters and all.

"It's not Kel's fault," I say. "So don't punish her. She . . . she does what Angel says."

'Cause I see it now, so clearly. It wasn't those two against me. It was never that. It was Angel against the world. And I should've got it ages ago, should've done what Randy did in the book – should've said I'm not showing up to the rumble. But I'm doing it now. And this way, this way there's a chance I can hold onto something, pull it out of the mess with me. Maybe. If Kel has the guts.

"Well, we'll talk to her in a moment," says Hopkins. "But what you've said certainly fits with what Mr MrCardle suggested. That you were put up to this."

"I . . ." And I don't what to say then. 'Cause of all the things I thought McCardle could have told Hopkins, I never expected that to be one of them. And I see then how stupid I was for thinking he was stupid. For thinking he'd give up on me. He never stopped believing in me. Not even when I stopped believing in myself.

"There will be consequences," Hopkins carries on. "For Asha, and the others. But we'll deal with those at a later date."

He stands and Otis stands too, grabs his hand and shakes it. Hopkins looks at it like he can't tell if it's been burned or blessed. I look over at Mum but she's looking out the window, like staring at the concrete will stop the tears. Otis helps her to her feet and nods at me to follow, but as I start to walk a voice stops me.

"Remember what I told you, Asha. About villains?"

And I don't turn round, but I know who's talking and I nod. "No moustaches," I say.

Just a tight top and fake lashes and blonde hair like spun sugar.

Nineteen

I don't know exactly what Kel says when she goes in later, but Hopkins calls and tells Otis that I'm only being suspended for two weeks, so I know she told the truth, and I know how much it's costing her and all. And I think that, of all the dares she's done – stealing cigarettes or snogging boys or scaling the walls of that house in Dulwich or the Castle pub – this was the biggest. And I didn't even have to Black Dare her, she did it all by herself.

And I want to dance then, I want to be in her

pinker than pink bedroom with Sharon's CDs on pretending we're Katy Perry and drinking Coke and laughing 'cause there's no more Angel telling us what we can and can't do and no more games and no more lies. It's over.

Only it's not, is it. 'Cause this wasn't just one bad thing, all wrapped up neat and dropped in the bin so no one can see anymore. It's more like chucking a stone into the pond on the Rye, it sends out ripples so everything feels it – from the litter bobbing at the edges to the turtles on the mud. And there's consequences, not just the ones Hopkins deals out and not just for me, but for Mum and Otis too.

I hear them that night, after Mum's done her shouting and wailing about being let down by me. After Otis has shaken his head so much I think his brain must hurt from banging on the sides. After Mum's vowed I'm not going back even after the suspension's over. After Otis has said that's not good for anything but her own satisfaction. After I've slunk to my bedroom so I don't have to see the ripples any more, sloshing against the walls of this too-small flat.

But like I say, I still hear them.

"I can't do this any more," she says. "I need help."

"You got me," he says. "We find a way, Chrissie."

"I'll be back at work soon enough," she says. "Money coming in, she can go back to proper school."

"Proper. Tsch. You mean private school. Same as before."

"No. A new one."

"Can't run for ever, chile," he says.

"I'm not your child," she says.

"You are to me," he says. "However hard you push."

Then there's quiet for a bit. But it's only so Otis can work it out. 'Cause a minute later I hear, "He didn't go, did he."

"What? Who?" she says.

But she knows who. And so do I. And I know Otis is right.

"Ellis didn't leave you," says Otis. "He didn't run. You push him."

And then I see it — the rowing, the doors slamming. It wasn't him fighting to go. He was fighting to stay.

"Better a push than wait for him to jump."

"Maybe he not the jumping type. Not all men like her father."

"They're not all like you either. Perfect Otis. Always doing the right thing. God always smiling on you."

"Ha." Otis lets out a laugh, big-barrelled and deep. "You think he smiling on me when he took your daddy? Then your mamma? They not just yours, chile. They mine too. You think I don't curse him for nearly taking you? Anyway, this not about me. This about you not needing anybody. Thinking you fine all by yourself. Well, look where that got you."

Mum's quieter now. "I will not be a burden."

"Maybe you not a burden. Maybe I need you. Like Asha need you. Like Ellis need you."

And that's the last thing either of them say. But they don't need to say anything else 'cause it's all clear now, what's happened and what I got to do to make it right, make it up to her, to all of them.

Twenty

I write the invites out with special ink pen on metallic paper I get down WHSmith on Tuesday, like it's a golden ticket, only to our flat not a chocolate factory, and there's no Oompa-Loompas or Willy Wonka or glass elevator, just a load of stairs and me and Mum and Otis. But I reckon that's enough.

I've said to come a week Sunday at four o'clock. A week after Mum's last chemo so she's past the being sick and being tired and maybe even past the hating me. And so she's had time to think about what Otis said too, so she's weighed up the arguments, used her judgement wisely. And even though I've told myself I'm stopping with all the stories and the wishing life was like on telly or in a magazine, in the end it really is like something out of a book, only you couldn't write it this well, not even if you were J.K. Rowling.

I've made two kinds of jelly and Otis has made lemon cake and seed cake and got Jaffa Cakes and party rings, and when Mum asks what we're up to, Otis tells her it's for Joe, 'cause he's coming to tea.

"That's a lot for a skinny thing," she says. "Anyway, I thought you weren't speaking to him, Asha."

"I changed my mind," I say.

I called him that night. Told him everything. And he didn't once get mad or call me out for lying to him or lying about him or for kissing Ronan Dooley. He just stayed quiet and let me talk, and when I was done he told me about this thing he'd seen on telly about what would happen if all the bees die and there might be a famine in some countries and how he's going to ask his mum if he can keep bees on the roof of their block of flats, and then I knew it was going to be all right.

He's the first to arrive and I'm tripping with nerves when I open the door – not the sick kind, the scared kind I had when I was running with Angel, but an alive feeling, like butterflies are beating their wings inside me, lifting me so I'm dizzy with it all. When I open the door he waits on the mat for a moment, on the landing where he used to live, and I realise how much guts it took to come back here that time when I was up West, more guts than me and the girls had.

And then the words that've been stuck in my throat for two weeks come bursting out, borne by admirals and peacocks and cabbage whites that fly off down past the Polish men and the Patels and Mrs Joyful King and her tea leaves, leaving me strong and sure of this.

"I'm sorry, Joe," I say.

He nods. "I know you are," he says. And I know then he never stopped believing in me either. And then I'm hugging him, and he's hugging me back, holding me tight, so tight I think he's trying to squeeze out the last of the bad, make sure I don't do it again, though I could've told him that I left that outside Hopkins' office the day I decided to tell the truth. Then Otis is calling him "son" and telling him to sit his behind down, and he's cutting him lemon cake and pouring him a glass of the cola Mum sucked her teeth at when we brought it home. And just as Joe's telling Mum his theory about the bees the doorbell goes again.

"Who's that now?" she asks.

Otis shrugs, busies himself with a teabag that don't need meddling with.

"Asha?"

I feel more butterflies "I— We invited some other people," I say.

She's looks over at Otis but he's still got his mind on the teabag so she flicks her eyes back on me and

I'm worried she's worked it out and it'll be over before it's even started. But in the end she just nods. "Well, go answer it then," she says.

"Why don't you go, Chrissie," Otis says. "Asha want to talk to Joe here."

Mum sucks her teeth like she never left SE15 and stands up, steadier now than she's been in months, her legs stronger and sleeker in proper tights instead of her old jogging bottoms. She looks fine, I think. We did her wig so it looks more real, and her eyebrows too and she got lipstick on. She didn't want it but I begged her, said it was just for fun and she rolled her eyes and pouted and I painted on this dark burgundy that shines like blackcurrant jam.

"Back to how it always was," she says, walking into the hall. "Mama doing the work." But I can tell she's smiling when she says it 'cause her voice is sing-song.

Joe reaches for my hand and I feel my face get hot 'cause Otis is watching, but Otis don't mind, he knows this isn't about us, it's about Mum.

I hear the door latch pull down and the door

swing open. Then I hear silence. Deafening again, thicker than butter.

Then his name.

"Ellis," she says. "Ellis." Like she's testing it out, like she almost forgot it and has found it shining again, like a penny once lost under the sofa where she let it roll.

He doesn't say hers back. He doesn't say anything. All we hear is the door close and then the quietness of two people standing and staring at each other in wonder. Then not even that, as Otis gets up and closes the door to the front room.

"Let them have some privacy," he says. "They got a lot to talk about."

And though not a word of it sneaks along the carpet or through the cracks, I know she's told him she made a mistake pushing him out and he's told her he shouldn't have let her. Maybe not those words, but something like them. Because soon the door opens again and Ellis is coming in and he's smiling wide, only not like the crocodile I thought he was

JOANNA NADIN

but a kinder animal, a dog maybe. She's not the tiger she used to be either, not broken like I thought she was, but just softer somehow, so that now I can see how they go together. And how I fit in.

"You done good, girl," she says to me.

And Ellis laughs and nods at me. And though he still don't know how to give me a hug, I know he's thinking about it and that's the first step, and we got a long time to make the rest.

But not today, today isn't for journeys, it's for enjoying this moment, for staying in, for partying, with a family made of jigsaw pieces that shouldn't slot together but somehow they do. And with a jumble of friends.

Patience is next. She comes with a bunch of flowers and biscuits from her Mum and forgiveness on her tongue, and I don't care if it's because God told her to or she just knew I needed it but she's my friend again and I am more grateful than if I'd won a week in Disney.

The doorbell goes again, hard and long, and I answer this time 'cause I'm pretty sure who this is going to be.

She's jigging on the landing, all skin and bones and nerves in a crop top and leggings and her hair in the fishtail plait I taught her.

Kelly.

"All right," I say.

"All right," she says back. And then next thing we're hugging and I feel her bony ribs and smell bubblegum and cheap body spray, and it's a good smell – of laughing on the back seat of a bus, and passing notes, and whispering about who we like. And then pull away, 'cause I know I got to say something, before she sees him again.

"Listen," I say. "You and Joe—"

But she don't let me finish. "It's fine," she says. "I thought about it and what he done – it was only what we done too, wasn't it. Telling the truth, I mean."

I nod. "Yeah," I say. "He's not so different, you know."

"I ain't told my mum, though." She laughs then, a nervous sound. "I will. Just, one thing at a time, you know."

I smile at her, then. And the boy standing all awkward just behind her with his hands in the pockets of his cords and a Big Bang T-shirt. "All right, Marvin," I say.

"All right," he says back.

Kel nudges him and he nudges her back, just like Joe does to me. And that makes me feel warm as anything.

"Listen," says Kel. "You sure your mum don't mind us being here."

I shake my head. "She don't mind."

And she don't. Not even when Marvin spills cola on the carpet and mops it up with a cushion 'cause he's so nervous. Not even when she can see the piercing in Kel's belly button and I know she's thinking I better not be thinking about getting one. Not even when Kelly swears and then swears again when she realises what she's said. 'Cause Mum knows what Kel did for me, and she knows what she lost because of it.

None of us mention her. Like she's the devil that can't be named; the friend who turned out to be the villain after all. But she's not a villain, not really, whatever McCardle thinks. Life's not as simple as it is in books. Good people do bad things, we all do. And baddies turn out to be heroes – or heroines. So she lied, but so did I. We all make up stories to make it better, to make life glitter and sparkle when really it's got gum stuck to it and it's frayed at the edges.

And that's when I hear it. The doorbell again. And I think, *I didn't invite no one else*, and I look over at Mum but she and Ellis talking about some case and arguing their points but in that way so's you know it's fun, not fighting, and Otis, he's showing Patience a card trick while Joe and Marvin and Kel take turns choosing songs on Kel's iPod.

So in the end I go, I slip out silent, smiling like that Cheshire Cat 'cause this really is a Wonderland right now.

253

But when I open the door the smile slips and Wonderland dissolves and I'm back to real life, and real life is that Angel is standing on the doorstep with a bag in her hand and a face on her like she's eaten a big fat slice of humble pie and it didn't go down too well.

"Asha," she says.

I don't say anything, 'cause I don't know what I'm supposed to say. I never written a scene like this one, and the ones in the books and films always got doors slamming, or kissing and making up, and I don't reckon I want to slam anything but I don't want to be BFFs neither.

"I got you something," she says, and holds out the bag.

I take it. And I don't look, but I know what it is.

"Thanks," I say.

"*De nada*," she says, and then she turns and is gone, said what she had to say, done what she had to do.

"*De nada,*" I say to her back as I watch it disappear down the stairwell.

But it isn't. It isn't nothing. Not for her.

I wait 'til the party's over and I'm in my room to open it. But I knew what was going to be in there anyway. It's a book. McCardle's book. Not the same one, exactly, 'cause that was old and worn. But a new one, all shiny and fresh from the shop. And I know how much it cost her – not to buy it, although that was £6.99 'cause she left the receipt in the bag and I know she don't like to spend money on anything that isn't wearable – but to do this for him, to admit she made a mistake.

"What you got there?"

I look up from my bed, and see Mum in the doorway.

"Just a book," I say, going to put it back in the bag. Only then I get an idea, an idea so golden, so bright I can't believe I never saw it, never thought of it before. "You want to hear it?" I ask.

And she does. She squashes up next to me on the bed, like she used to when I was little. Only this time it's me reading her a bedtime story, just like Ponyboy read *Gone With the Wind* to Johnnycake. I read her all about them two, and about Sodapop and Darry too, who acts the father, because there isn't a real one about, all yelling at him, "Where you been?" Only Ponyboy realises Darry's not angry really. He's worried. He's really saying, "Be careful, because I couldn't stand it if anything happened to you."

And when I get to that bit she nods, squeezes my leg that's lying on the bed next to her. And I know what that squeeze is saying. It's saying, "That's what I felt." Because she wasn't a tiger no more, she couldn't protect me. So she just shouted instead.

Then it squeezes again and I know what this means too. It means, read on, chile.

And I do, I read every night that week, until I read the last words, and start on a new book that she got from the library when she went out for a walk with

Mrs Joyful King. But I don't put this one away on my shelf. I open up the inside cover and I write a message. *Stay gold, Ponyboy*, I write. Then I sign my name, just like T. Lutter did. And I don't know who he was, but I bet he was clever, and I want to be like him, or her. And like McCardle and all. I'll give it to him, I think. On the first day back.

'Cause I'm going back.

Mum wasn't happy. She'd rung Haberdashers' and a place was coming up in a month when some girl was moving up North 'cause her dad had bought a factory. But I told her I didn't want it. There's no point. Angel's not coming back. Her mum's pulled her out saying there's too much bad influence, so she's the one's going to end up at Haberdashers'. Good luck to her. Besides, school's school wherever you go. There's always going to be Angels: Girls who got snakes for tongues. Girls who make you look in the mirror so you can see you're not the fairest of them all. Girls who give you three wishes only they turn out to be curses and you're stuck in the same old story. Only difference is they're wearing Prada, not Primark.

But there's always going to be good kids too. Ones like Kel who make you laugh, who make you realise family's everything, even if it's not the one you thought you had. Or like Patience who always look out for you even when you don't once look out for them, look at them. Or like Joe, kids who'll wait for you to test out being another girl, just for a bit, before you realise the one you started out as wasn't that bad after all.

The trouble is working out which is which, 'cause they don't wear badges.

But back at the party, when I look at Kel dancing to old reggae on the record player, and Marvin teaching Joe how to solve a Rubik's Cube, and Patience on her third helping of cake and not even once caring whether it's going to her hips or her thighs, I reckon I'm getting there.

'Cause they all got adventure in them. And maybe their lives won't get made into books or films, but they're still worth telling, worth being a part of. So I'm doing what Ponyboy did. I'm thinking up a new story now, about a girl like me. Only she's not secretly a spy or a detective or a superhero saving the world, she just has to get through her first term at a new school.

I reckon that's enough story for anyone.

Acknowledgements

With thanks to my agent Julia Churchill who dropped the seed "black dare" casually into conversation the first time we met, never imagining it would grow into a book. To Karen Ball at Little, Brown for championing Asha and Joe and me. To the doctoral writing group at Bath Spa University who renamed Patience. To the Thinkers, for never running out of wise words. And to Peckham, which will always be some kind of home.

Discover Joe's story in *Joe All Alone*

NO PARENTS, NO RULES...
NO PROBLEM?

JOE ALL ALONE

JOANNA NADIN

Available now